SOUTH OF DODGE

Could just one man survive the challenge of taking on Morro City, plagued as it was with unsolved murders? That was the doubt dogging tough investigator Chad Brodie as he rode into town to take on a task that seemed impossible. The law had been defied and good men lay in their graves. Soon Brodie would find himself alone and pitted against both a formidable town and a bloody land haunted by outlaws. He would bring peace to the territory – or die in the attempt.

SOUTH OF DODGE

SOUTH OF DODGE

by

Nick Benjamin

Dales Large Print Books
Long Preston, North Yorkshire,
BD23 4ND, England.

British Library Cataloguing in Publication Data.

Benjamin, Nick
    South of Dodge.

    A catalogue record of this book is
    available from the British Library

    ISBN   1-84262-435-0 pbk

First published in Great Britain 2005 by Robert Hale Limited

Cover illustration © Longarron by arrangement with
Norma Editorial S.A.

Published in Large Print 2006 by arrangement with
Robert Hale Ltd.

Dales Large Print is an imprint of Library Magna Books Ltd.

Printed and bound in Great Britain by
T.J. (International) Ltd., Cornwall, PL28 8RW

CHAPTER 1

SHOOTER'S DAY

There it was again.

A rustle of uneasiness seemed to stir the deep shadows surrounding the livery, yet he'd just checked the stables out a minute before and found them empty. Brodie, crouched low with his cocked .45 in his fist and every sense tinglingly alert, wanted to follow his hunch and move on to search for his quarry in that alley ahead beyond the lighted bath-house. But what if that slight sound proved not to be just a whisper of the wind, but rather six feet of desperado easing himself into position to cut loose with both barrels?

He shook his curly head.

No. Go with your first instincts, Brodie. It's no more than twenty feet to the alleymouth with its welcoming, enveloping shadows...

He was actually rising from his crouch when Fowler's big .44 opened up like cannon fire from the livery, sending racketing waves of sound rolling down the falsefronted canyon of Drinkwater Street.

The range detective's lightning reflexes saw him dive behind the cover of the water trough as the wild-eyed badman was momentarily framed in the stable doorway, .44 barking like a savage dog and lead ripping up furrows of dust everyplace other than in the immediate vicinity of the trough.

This wild spraying of bullets was about the only encouraging feature of Jim Fowler's gunplay from the point of view of any man reckless enough to go after him for the reward. The outlaw was mean and vicious with a record as long as your arm, but as a guntipper he simply did not rate. It was this well-known factor, as much as any other reason, which had encouraged down-on-his-luck Brodie to go after the perpetrator of the Hoganville bank job, a one-man manhunt which had thus far chewed up three weeks of his time, but which now looked like bearing fruit – providing Fowler didn't get lucky and aim one straight.

The doorway of the bath-house beckoned from close by. Brodie was up, lunging for it. The outlaw screamed an obscenity, rested his smoking Colt barrel on his left forearm, drew a careful bead on the lithe, fast-stepping figure and gently squeezed trigger.

Brodie could have laughed in relief as a lighted window, a good ten feet distant, went out with a splintering crash. Then he was safely through the door and heeled it closed behind him.

His grin vanished as the corner of his eye caught the heavy object hurtling at his head.

'What in the sweet blue hell...?'

He ducked, and not a moment too soon. The heavy bathroom pitcher whistled over his curving back to shatter against the bureau as the bird-naked bather leapt from her bubble bath, reaching for the towel rack.

A lesser man might have been diverted. But not a hungry Chad Brodie, poised on the brink of finalizing his first successful job all winter. Over the past weeks he'd trailed one of the territory's most wanted across a hundred miles of frozen country, had survived ambush, blizzard, landslide and a hair-raising pursuit by a bunch of starving timber-wolves up on Sinner's Mountain. Now Fowler was his, and not even this sublime apparition of terrified and outraged femininity, all pink and steaming and indignantly jiggling here before him in the warm glow of the Hoganville bath-house could delay him longer than maybe one jaw-hanging moment.

But much could happen in even that slice of time, particularly if you happened to be a desperado on the run with a $10,000 bank haul stashed someplace in the Shirreff's Wastes, a bullet in your shoulder, a hard-nosed manhunter pressing you hard and an entire town rooting for your demise.

Hoofbeats.

Brodie leapt erect.

Fowler had got a horse underneath him!

This was largely a stroke of badman's luck insofar as every horse but Mace O'Hare's appaloosa had snapped its tie-reins and bolted as soon as shooting broke out. But luck in the shape of a buffalo-hunter's cayuse, trained not to be gun-shy, was there outside the hotel, and the killer had streaked along the street to fill the appaloosa's saddle and get it running even as Brodie lunged from the bath-house door.

Then the unexpected.

Pallid light glinted on gunmetal and powder-smoke billowed whitely from the hitherto deserted saloon porch across the street in the same moment that Brodie reappeared on the walk and the mounted badman raked horsehide with spur.

Brodie's jaw sagged in disbelief as he

watched the bulky, bald-domed figure of the sheriff, face red with rage, jack a spent shell from his huge buffalo gun and lever another into the chamber.

'No!' he roared as the appaloosa began picking up real speed. He waved his arms frantically. 'Leave him to me, damn you. He's got to be taken al–'

His voice was downed by gun thunder. Not even quivering outrage could diminish the lawman's marksmanship. He could pick off a horsefly on a buffalo's rump at a hundred yards with his trusty Big Fifty. His first shot had fanned Fowler's devilish black mustache, and though the wild-eyed bad-man ducked and screamed into the horse's ear and jerked its head frantically first left and then right, that second bullet seemed as inevitable as destiny itself as it sped to its mark as though guided by Justice's steady hand.

In an instant the saddle was empty and the buffalo hunter's well-disciplined mount quickly broke back to a trot and began circling round for the saloon. Sheriff O'Hare was lowering his gun with an air of grim satisfaction as the first awed citizen poked his head from a window to stare along Drinkwater Street at the motionless figure sprawled on its back in the reddening mud, arms out-flung, shirt unbuttoned in defiance of the elements and handsome head canted grace-fully to one side as though he were sleeping.

But bad Jim Fowler was stone dead, as anybody could see, and the cheering was already beginning as a bitter-lipped Brodie shook his head, leaned a weary hand against an upright and completed his interrupted sentence in a hollow voice: 'Alive.'

He'd not only wanted to bring Fowler in alive; it was essential. The president of the Hoganville bank had posted $1000 on the bandit's head but this was conditional on his being delivered alive in order that he might be forced to reveal where he had stashed the ten grand.

Dead, the badman was worth the big zero. Which was roughly what Warrior Creek's range detective was worth at that moment as the first jubilant towner came rushing up to shake him by the hand for tracking the outlaw for a hundred miles and hazing him right back to Hoganville where the sheriff could rightly claim his scalp.

For just a moment that emotional citizen might have been perilously close to joining Fowler on his final journey.

'Hey, ain't that Brodie?'

'Ain't sure ... all huddled up like that. But wait a minute ... yeah, it's our boy right enough. Hey, everybody, it's the hero hisself back safe and sound. Chad, wait up a minute!'

The trim figure in Warrior Creek's drizzling night, with jacket collar turned well up round chilled ears, suddenly lengthened his stride as men came rushing towards him, but he was blocked by a fat storekeeper who threw his arms wide as though welcoming home the prodigal son.

'Chad, Chad,' the man beamed. 'Who said you was all through? We knew you could do it, no matter what the papers are saying about no money for you. They had the army, the marshals, the goddamn Injun trackers and half the lawmen in the county out after that Fowler, but it was Warrior Creek's best man that bagged him. C'mon, give the man room, you fellers,' he yelled, seizing Brodie's elbow with a proprietary hand. 'Let's get inside where it's warm, boy, and you can tell us all exactly how you done it.'

Somehow Brodie managed to endure the following half-hour during which Delaney's store filled to bursting-point with admirers all eager to welcome him back and pay homage. Vocal homage, that was. Not a man of them seemed to think he might be in need of shot, a bag of biscuits, or most important of all, some folding green. Why should they? He was the hero of the hour, wasn't he? A man didn't insult a genuine hero by offering handouts the way you might to some panhandling bum. Not in Warrior Creek they didn't.

There was a heavy feeling of *déjà vu* weighing him down as he eventually escaped the last back-slapper to make his way along the overcrowded street, collar turned up again, battered ten-gallon tugged low.

This was not the first time the man who did business from a two-room office identified by a scarred brass plate bearing the brave words BRODIE INVESTIGATIONS had seen success and acclaim. Last year he'd investigated, solved and brought to justice those responsible for the kidnapping of a wealthy cattle baron from over Palmito way. He'd shot it out with the Hanrahan boys in a hell-hole saloon at Virgil River in the spring and netted a $200 reward for the successful tracking down of Chief Walking Wizard the Osage who simply found himself unable to surrender his old scalp-lifting ways when the Bluecoats took over.

He had enjoyed publicity before and had

seen his likeness blazoned on Page 1 of the *Word Warrior* newspaper, and from time to time had had impressionable women lusting after him in light of some achievement which thrust him into the limelight.

He sighed. Islands of achievement dotted sparsely across an ocean of no-income months, bean sandwiches, cheap booze, too many failures and plain bad luck. And, of course, ongoing accommodation problems.

It seemed to Chad Brodie on a bitter sweet night like this that the greatest difficulty he'd encountered since nailing up his shingle had not been the vengeful guns of those he hunted, the baking desert heat or winter snows of the long manhunting trails, but rather the mundane and ongoing problem of maintaining a roof over his head.

Cowboys had bunkhouses, tycoons had stately mansions, shoe-clerks had their little one-roomers and some fast women of his acquaintance had carpets on their floors and frilly lace curtains at the windows.

He slept on a hard, pull-down bunk behind his desk at 32 Westbank Avenue, where the roof leaked and the roaches roamed free. He was classified as a self-employed business-man so nobody was responsible for paying him a wage when things were slow. Yet B.B.B.

15

Realty, his mysteriously invisible landlords, demanded their exhorbitant rental fee every single week come rain or come shine.

And his inner self groaned. One thousand greenback dollars!

That was what he'd missed out on when a drum-gutted badgeman with a Big Henry that couldn't miss drilled a neat round hole in Fowler's skinny back and blasted a big chunk of his heart through the gaping exit hole in his chest on Hoganville's Drinkwater Street.

Had the reward money been paid he could have caught up on his arrears and even paid the faceless men of B.B.B. a month's rent in advance – two or three months if he'd wanted. Could have sent them flowers with an ambiguous note attached: *May you enjoy Death as much as I enjoy life.* Or perhaps: *The prophet warns; protect your ass at all times.*

He knew he was feeling down whenever his thoughts wandered this way. And it was almost like conceding defeat when he found himself thinking in terms of blackjack, poker and dice. He'd made his living briefly with the cards before setting his sights on higher things, namely a range detective's diploma issued by the Kansas Marshals' office. A dozen times since he'd sworn off the tables for keeps, only to find himself backsliding to the cards and horses simply in order to maintain his modest premises at Westbank Avenue and keep his dream alive.

He felt he'd almost been able to feel the fat comforting weight of that $1,000 fee in his hip pocket right up until the very moment that buffalo gun had roared out to reduce his prospects to zero.

Now with the excitement fading, he was back in Warrior Creek, it was raining and he was standing out front of his up-a-flight premises with water trickling down his back and reality weighing heavier upon him than ever before.

Home was the hero – and he couldn't stand here all night.

The stairs creaked familiarly under his weight and the customary dribbles were coming through the uncaulked tin roof. He let himself in, made a light then turned to stare at the envelope he knew would be there on the floor just inside his door.

He had never met his landlords. He paid his rent to a box at the post office where confidentiality was sacrosanct. He ripped the envelope open and read;

You are no hero to us.
Meet your arrears or taste our wrath.
The Lord detests the malefactor.

He grunted as he took a bottle from a cupboard and dropped into a beat-up chair. For some perverse reason he almost enjoyed his anonymous, insult-ridden relationship with his landlords whoever they might be.

From the outset of his tenancy, B.B.B. had treated him like a loser, and he believed he'd stayed on at 32 Westbank as much to achieve real success and flaunt it in their unknown faces as for any other reason. But having had that possibility slip through his fingers at Hoganville the way it had done, he realized with sudden clarity now as he swallowed a draft of cheapest rotgut, that this was the last straw.

He'd battled with Lady Luck, mad-dog gun hellions and greedy landlords for far too long, simply to enable himself to continue following the only profession that interested him. He had fought the good fight longer than almost anyone expected. But only a punch-drunk fighter would keep stepping into the ring when he knew he was all through.

A drop of freezing rainwater fell on his

bare head as he raised his glass in mocking salute to the brass sign upon his open door. This range detective was finally all through. First thing tomorrow he would canvass the saloons in search of a job. As a dealer. He was as good with the cards and dice as he was at taming rowdy drunks or gun-happy hellions, and such local luminaries as Fat Max, Big Jilly and Morey Silverburg were always putting out overtures for his specialist services.

He slept in his chair that night and dreamed yet again of the successful Big Job that always eluded him. He feared that special dream would continue to haunt his nights long after he'd finally called it quits.

The rain had disappeared overnight and the morning was sunny if cold as the lone horseman appeared over the rim leading into Warrior Creek. This was a rough workngman's place, a town with broad shoulders and whiskey on its breath, where dudes were few and far between and men who sported jewellery and a diamond finger-ring even scarcer. A bunch of day laborers unloading a freighter in Wheelahan's goods yard paused to appraise the newcomer, yet despite his immaculate rig and the obvious quality of the buckskin he rode, this man was allowed to pass by without the whistle or the derisive comment, something which might have puzzled the casual observer, but not such men as the sheriff or the swamper at the Daybreak saloon, who also paused to give this one a good looking-over.

You simply didn't razz a stranger like this. It was that simple. His breed could sport lace shirtfronts and smell like a perfumery if they wanted, and only a fool would go out of his way to aggravate them. For his shoulders were wide, his back arrogantly straight and beneath an immaculately tailored riding-coat was strapped a double gunrig from which thrust a pair of ivory-handled Smith & Wesson .38 revolvers, cartridge rims reflecting thin sunlight.

But more than the trappings, it was Murch Chisum's air of self-assurance that made the deepest impression. He met each curious searching eye boldly and returned the look with steely arrogance. Such men, the wise ones of Warrior Creek knew, were always best left alone, and as he rode on by about all they were left to do was speculate on just who or what he might be.

Lawman was a possibility, although nobody knew any peace officer who wore fifty-dollar jackets and hundred-dollar boots. Nor did he appear to fit the mold of gunfighter, outlaw or itinerant gambler. He looked nothing like a drummer and seemed far too cocky and full of himself simply to be a businessman, so what did that leave?

There was only one citizen in town who knew exactly who and what Chisum the private investigator was, and that was Warrior Creek's stony-broke hero of the hour. The two went quite a way back, and indeed it was Brodie's presence in the town that was the reason for the stranger's appearance today, as the sheriff quickly found out when the new arrival dismounted, tied up at the jailhouse hitch rail and presented himself at the jail-house door.

'Evening, Sheriff,' he said politely, doffing his hat. 'Could you tell me where I might find Mr Chad Brodie, the range detective?'

'Sure can, stranger,' the lawman supplied. 'Mostly if he ain't off on a job you'd find him round at his office on Westbank Avenue, but right now he's almost certain to be at Big Jilly's on Main, either helping keep the wild boys in order or more'n likely upstairs bucking the tiger.'

The big man frowned faintly. 'Gambling?'

'Reckon so. You a friend of his, mister?'

'That's a moot question, Sheriff.'

'Is it?' replied the law, wondering what in hell 'moot' might mean. 'Well, anyways, Jilly's is your best bet and...'

His voice trailed off. The stranger had turned his broad back and walked away.

'Well, good night to you too, pilgrim,' the sheriff said testily, and banged his door and went back to his coffee.

It was cold.

Brodie was ahead twenty dollars.

Brodie was about even.

Brodie was down ten bucks he couldn't afford and wondering if he should risk one more hand.

'Goin' again, Chad?' the dealer asked from beneath his black-billed cap.

He rose and shook his head. 'Maybe later, Rico.'

'Yeah, Chad, later. So here they go round and round again, boys, look at 'em and weep.'

He turned his back on the six desperates hunched around Rico's table like buzzards at an overripe kill, absently took out his makings.

He looked bad and knew it as he went looking for Big Jilly.

Usually impressively self-assured and stylish even on his bad days, Brodie today was a changed man. Disappointment and a night spent slumped in a rickety office chair as he worked his way through half a fifth of Bottled in the Barn aggravated by the fact that he had not shaved or changed before drifting down to drop in on Big Jilly at the Rough Rider looking for a job or to augment his luck – all combined to ensure that he looked like twenty miles of bad road exactly when he might have wanted to look at his most successful, buoyant best. Big Jilly didn't care how in hell he looked. He'd had Brodie boss his tables several times and knew he would prove a greater asset to the Rough Rider full time even than Libby Finemore, the big-breasted dancing sensation he'd just imported from Capital City.

Both men were unaware of the town's mid-morning arrival as they sat at Jilly's private table by the piano. The saloonkeeper was sucking on a fuming corona but Brodie was yet to light up his first of the day in deference to a throat affected by too much cheap tobacco.

'The job is yours, Chad. It's always been yours. Seems I recollect comin' to you the day after you set up shop to offer you regular wages. Figured you were makin' a wrong move after doin' that course in detectivin' down South, but it looks like it took more'n a year to prove me right, huh?'

Chad Brodie had one of those boyishly rugged Western faces with broad bone-structure, solid jaw, wide-set blue eyes beneath dark brows, a broad forehead that spoke of intelligence and a mouth set in a way that warned of a testy temperament.

At that moment his features were expressionless, while behind blue eyes he was imagining how sweet it would be to upend two-fifty pound Jilly and ram his fat head into one of his spittoons.

Although flattering him and offering him a paying job, the saloon boss was enjoying this, he knew. Reminding him he'd crapped out. Rubbing it in that he'd warned him he could not make a success as a range detective or private investigator in a place like this.

Soon, Brodie knew, he would be dealing with similar snide attitudes from bums, deadbeats and barflies to whom he must turn a deaf ear. For from time to time in this town Brodie had ridden tall and sometimes cocky. They'd admired him for that but, being human, they would also relish the spectacle of his being dragged down off his high horse to something more like their level.

He could take that. He had no option.

'When?' he grunted.

'Huh?'

'When do I start?'

Jilly spread hands wide, his fat little fingers like sausages with glistening nails which his bargirl polished for him along with anything else that needed it.

'What's wrong with today?' Then he leaned forward and said seriously, 'But it might be an idea to go home and spruce up first, pal. No offence, but the truth is you look more like a bum you might be called on to throw out than a table captain. OK?'

Brodie was already earning his money before he'd even kicked one wild cowboy through the batwings or caught some card-slick augmenting his luck. He told himself he welcomed it. The quicker he got to living and thinking like a wage-plugger the less painful it would be in the long run.

'You've got a deal,' he muttered, then turned sharply at the sound of a voice and looked up sharply at a smiling clean shaven face. 'Goddamn!'

'And a big howdy to you too, Chad,' laughed the urbane newcomer. He doffed his hat and smiled at the saloonkeeper. 'Mr

Jilly, I believe. I'm Murchell Chisum from Dodge City, general investigator, at your service. We'll have two glasses of your best brown ale and a little privacy, thank you.'

Big Jilly knew when he was being talked down to. He heaved his bulk erect in a huff, red-faced and peeved as he collected his pocket flint from the table.

'Another investigator, huh? And a friend of yours eh, Chad? Well, hope this don't get to be a habit ... got to keep the tone of the Rider in mind, you know. Great meetin' you, Mr Dick. Hey, Jenny, two cold ones for two make-believe lawmen when you're ready.'

'Charming friends you have, Chad,' Chisum murmured as he filled the owner's chair and placed his hat on the table between them. He stripped off riding-gloves with a faint frown. 'I hate to say it, but you look lousy. I hope I haven't made this journey for nothing. You are still, er, capable, I take it?'

Brodie decided it was time for the first smoke of the day and to hell with the raspy throat.

He remained silent as his deft fingers built tobacco and rice-paper into a perfect cylinder which he licked into shape with the tip of his tongue. It was true what they said, he mused. Things were never so bad they could not get worse. He'd have rather faced Jesse James in a bad mood, the I.R.S. and even B.B.B. and associates all together than this smoothly impressive man from the north. For Murch Chisum was exactly what he so desperately wanted to be, not just an investigator and range detective but a highly successful one.

The two went back quite a ways.

Chisum was already established and prospering in his chosen profession when a youthful Brodie made his own unlikely start in the sleuthing business.

It began when his parents were fleeced on a property deal and he took up the cudgels on their behalf, prying, investigating, bullying when it was called for and bribing officials when there was no other recourse until he had enough to drag the sharpsters into court, and won.

Up until that point Brodie had been content to drift, gamble, take what romance or action came along and in general enjoyed a wasteful if high-paced life. Yet a part of his nature had always rebelled at injustice and the stink of exploitation or crooked dealing. The experience with his parents aroused his ideals, and when he chanced to come into contact with an investigator working for Chisum, he went looking for a job, and to his surprise, landed it.

Chisum paid him lousy money to learn the business from the ground up, and more often than not Brodie found himself working as bodyguard, troubleshooter, escort and hired muscle rather than at the brainy end of the business.

Yet he picked up a great deal and achieved some small successes in the investigative field before the relationship turned sour. Innately arrogant and authoritative, the mercurial Chisum in time appeared to feel threatened by Brodie's ever widening skills, ranging from his investigative work to a genuine talent with a Colt .45.

Things hadn't been helped along any when the whisper went round that Chisum's glamorous wife had some sort of crush on her husband's apprentice, even if Brodie was unaware of that fact.

Came the parting of the ways and Brodie hadn't seen his former tutor and boss since, until today. And he knew, even before Chisum really got down to business that it hadn't been chance that brought him here. Chisum did nothing by chance or accident. In business he believed in sizing up a given

28

situation, lining up the talent to deal with it, then going in hard, with winning the only acceptable outcome.

With a woman involved in their last head-to-head, their parting had been acrimonious, with Chisum predicting his former assistant would be lucky to survive three months on his own. He'd survived fifteen actually, but only just. Now he was all through. And of all the lousy days he'd endured since hanging his shingle in Warrior Creek, Chisum had had to select this one to stop by. The first big drag on his durham caused him to cough and see little black dots floating past his eyes. But he still felt better as he sat up straighter, squared his shoulders and thrust out a jaw every bit as aggressive and flinty as the other's.

'What do you want, big man? And don't tell me you just happened by, as I'll know it's a lie.'

The girl arrived with the beer. She was young and buxom and gave Brodie a warm smile as she set the glasses down. She liked him and never made any attempt to hide it. She sniffed disapprovingly at Chisum as she turned away with a supple roll of neat hips. This slick stranger looked too top-lofty and full of himself for Jenny's earthy tastes.

'Are you still working?' Chisum asked brusquely.

'Sure,' he lied. He was half-hoping the other might just visit and get gone without learning the truth. 'Why wouldn't I be?'

'Hmm, still handling the truth carelessly, I see.' Chisum sampled his beer and jerked a thumb. 'The doorman told me you've shut up shop. He doesn't like you, Chad. Must be scared you'll take his job or something. Now, do you think we can talk straight for a change? You're all washed up and looking for a payday, correct?'

Brodie swallowed both beer and pride. He had a headache and he hated Chisum's guts because he had everything and he had nothing. So what? Life went on.

'You know all the answers, like always. So I'll ask you one more time, what are you doing in Warrior Creek?'

The big man's smile was malicious.

'I could be playing Santa Claus, Chad, it's round that time of year.'

'Sure you could.'

'I mean it.' The smirk faded as Chisum rearranged his features into hard planes and angles, as formidable a face as a man might encounter anyplace. 'Brodie,' he said. No 'Chad' now. Suddenly he sounded just like

30

an employer interviewing a prospective employee. He wore a silk shirt with solid silver bola tie while Brodie sported denim opened at the neck. 'As you're aware I'm always a busy man and never more so than now. I've more clients than I can hope to handle even with my large staff.'

He enumerated on his fingers.

'I've two fraud cases under investigation, a kidnapping, several missing persons, a major rustling–'

'If you're offering something, do it. And skip the promoting, mister. I've heard it all before, remember? This big talk could mean you're rolling in it or are stony-broke. And whichever it is, it doesn't impress me.'

'If only that were true, Brodie. I can see you're every bit as envious and jealous of my success as you were when I took you off that job riding shotgun for Butterfield and put you to work in my outfit to pay for your course tuition in our trade. I guess a year and a half haven't changed anything. You're still a loser and a saloon-lizard at heart, aren't you?'

Brodie's knuckles wanted to smash something, while his features remained blank. He was thinking that, despite their differences, Chisum had played a part in his struggle to make something of himself up at Dodge City when he'd offered a position plus tutelage in his profession to someone who up until that point had many impressive skills but not a single one specifically.

For instance, handling bookkeeping at Chisum's big office in Dodge had been an eye-opener and life-changer for him. He'd proved to be a natural with figures to both his own surprise and Chisum's. He saw how profits were made and how almost everyone on the lower south side of the capital was in debt to Chisum and others like him. He saw how the man's ancillary businesses reached out and gathered in all the wool and grain, the hides and pelts and laid a lien on such things as cattle, sheep and land.

Chisum was highly successful even then but chose to put his profits into the store rather than in the crime-solving arms of Chisum Enterprises.

A store was solid, and it meant ongoing power and profit. It held men by catering to their needs, conning them with gimcracks and dazzling them with luxuries.

But it was also a safe occupation, rock-solid safe and secure compared with the always uncertain life of the range detective. Chisum had gotten shot up once while

Brodie was still working at the store, ambushed by a bunch of horse-thieves at Alpaca Pass in the Crystal Prairies region. Almost died. He later promoted apprentice Brodie from bookkeeping to investigative legwork while he recovered. A more cautious man when he recovered, maybe, but still more than a match for almost anyone in or out of the business, including himself.

Brodie stubbed out his butt in a brass ashtray.

He was looking at everything with a cold objective eye now. Had to. It would be better for himself if he simply acknowledged that this man was a huge success in the profession that had bested him, and accept it. He believed Chisum had come to offer him something and that he should grab it with both hands. Swallow the digs and the barbs, Brodie. There could be a lot worse fates than taking money and crap from Chisum. Sitting here, he only had to look around to see it.

'Whatever you say, big man, mister,' he ground out. 'Once a loser always a loser.' He paused, then had to add, 'But a tough loser, right?'

'I'll concede that,' the other replied soberly. 'You are tough, Brodie. No real brain for investigative work, and handicapped by envy of your betters, but you are surely tough enough by any yardstick.' A pause. 'I have work for a tough man with detective credentials and skills.'

Despite himself Chad felt a surge of interest. So he was right. Chisum had something in mind for him!

'Well?' Chisum demanded. 'Interested or not?'

'How big?'

'Very big.'

'Good money?'

'The best.'

'Then how come you're not taking it on yourself?'

It seemed to Brodie that Chisum flushed a little at that, but his response was firm and convincing.

'Two reasons. One, I've too much on my plate already. The other? This is a job suited more to a rough-case than a top investigator, as you'll find out if you take it on. Do I make myself plain?'

Brodie swallowed another chunk of humble-pie. He nodded.

'So, what sort of job is it anyway?'

Chisum leaned forward, expression intent. 'What do you know about counterfeiting?'

Brodie looked blank.

'As I calculated,' Chisum said acerbically. 'Nothing. Well,' what do you know about the undertaking business?'

Chad just shook his head.

'We've a lot of work to do,' Chisum stated brusquely. 'Before you leave for Morro I expect you to be at least familiar with both professions. We'll get started on you right away.'

And they did.

He was to learn that Chisum wasn't stretching the truth when he warned it was a big job.

CHAPTER 2

THE MORRO CONNECTION

There had been a time when undertaker Wilson Priest would only show up at the Bicknell spread outside Morro when some unlucky cowpoke or other had cashed in his chips. On those occasions the tall and balding Priest kept pretty much to himself, handled everything with solemn dignity and as a result was usually first choice when it came time for folks hereabouts to engage undertaking services for the victims of age, cholera and gunfights along with the inevitable accidents and plagues.

But times had changed.

These days Wilson Priest himself was far less available. He spent little time at his funeral parlor, had built himself a fine new home just outside Morro and boasted the most impressive rosewood carriage and matched bays to be seen in the entire county. He insisted that the cause of his sudden affluence was the result of canny investment in stocks and bonds, and who would doubt the word of such a solid citizen? Who would have the reason or nerve to do so?

So it came as some surprise when the undertaker showed up unannounced at the spread early that chilly morning astride his big new Arab, and the rancher would be mildly peeved when he heard the reason behind the visit.

The spread's living-quarters for the men were just a plain saddlebag bunkhouse, with bunk-room and kitchen divided by a roofed-over dogtrot which was open at either end.

The unsuspecting cook showed the visitor through to the bunk-room, where waddies were finishing off shaving and rigging up

36

before descending on the kitchen for flap-jacks and maple syrup. One man was buckling on his boots, another checking out the result of his shaving job in a small mirror nailed to the wall. There were six cowhands riding for the brand and the normally aloof undertaker greeted them all with a warm smile as he came in off the dogtrot.

'Morning, boys,' he said as they turned to study him in some surprise. He rubbed his hands together briskly and shivered. 'Not much of a morning to be out dragging fool cows out of half-frozen creeks before there's any real warmth in the sun, eh?'

Glances were exchanged. These were simple hardworking range hands accustomed to dull routine. The unannounced presence of the undertaker made them feel uneasy, reminding them of Old Man Death, so beloved by singers of cowboy ballads. The cocky, sway-backed young bronco-buster didn't look cocky any more, and the beanpole roper with the bright yellow hair opened his mouth as if to reply but closed it again. Distanced from this man by both his profession and new wealth, most had never even spoken with Wilson Priest before and were content to leave it that way.

'No sir,' affirmed the visitor, stamping

about as though concerned about frostbitten toes. 'Has to be easier ways for a man to make a living. Ah, don't you agree, Quint?'

Quint, the junior bronco-buster blinked in puzzlement. 'Guess so...'

'You know so, boy,' insisted Priest. 'And do you know where you can get a job for half again the money Mr Bicknell can afford to pay you, plus better conditions and at least half your time working indoors out of the weather. You only get one guess.'

Suddenly they understood.

These had been strange and eventful times in Morro County of late, times which had seen such violent affairs as gunfights, ambushes and at least one fatality in what until recently had been a generally lazy, and peace-loving kind of community. The man who'd lost his life, as all five hands seemed to remember at once; had been one of Priest Funerals' employees. The husky grave-digger-cum-roustabout, Digger Lassen, had been shot to death in a dust-up out at Frog Hollow several weeks earlier, resulting in Priest being left shorthanded.

Even in a community where regular jobs could be hard to come by, there was never any kind of rush to go to work for an undertaker.

'No way,' insisted the burly roper, an emphatic gesture accompanying his words. 'Sorry, you come to the wrong place, Mr Priest. Reckon as how none of us have got nothing against your perfession but I guess there ain't nobody here's got any kind of hankerin' to learn the croakin' trade neither.'

Priest launched into his pitch but it was obvious he was making no headway when the cook banged a wagon-tire to announce grub call. This offered hands the excuse and opportunity to jam hats on heads and go hustling out with a relieved clatter of boot-heels, happy to escape from sharing a confined space with a man who dealt in death.

Although as reverent as a hardshell preacher-man when engaged in the business of laying some citizen to rest, Priest had a lurid vocabulary which he was exercising as he moved back into the dogtrot, where he suddenly found himself confronted by the ranch foreman.

'Mr Bicknell wants to see you at the house, Mr Priest,' the man said. 'Pronto.'

Bicknell was a blocky fellow with a black spade beard who favored calico vests and rawhide galluses that held up his baggy jeans. The undertaker located him on his side porch with the sleeves of his hickory

39

shirt rolled up over beefy forearms, lathering his hands in a tin dish with a thick yellow bar of home-made soap.

The rancher didn't mince words. He could sympathize with Priest's situation in the wake of Van Lassen's death, he stated testily, but that didn't give the undertaker the right to come out here uninvited to try and poach his crew, and he would thank him to remember that.

A year back Wilson Priest would have accepted such a rebuke with stubborn but polite silence. Goodwill was important to an undertaker, particularly in a place like Morro where Priest Funerals had competition. But this newly affluent undertaker was a very different man, showed it in the way he stood his ground and insisted he had the democratic right of freedom of movement and could and would seek hired help just wherever he goddamn pleased.

The rancher flared up and advanced a couple of steps, drying his hands on a big rough towel. Priest stood his ground and suddenly Bicknell halted uneasily, not quite liking what he saw in the undertaker's eye.

'Goldurn it, Wilson Priest,' he complained, 'everyone's complainin' that your paper-shovin' on the stock market's gone

40

and changed you for the worst, and damned if I don't think they could be right. Why man, you are standin' here on my property with a look on your face like you would just as soon bust a man one instead of talkin' a thing through calm and easy like we always used to. Better get a hold of yourself and shuck some of your newfangled high and mighty ways while you still got any friends, mister, that's my advice to you.'

'And my advice to you is to go–' Priest began hotly but bit the words off. He spun and went striding off to the hitch rack. The black whickered a greeting but he just flung his heavy body astride and rode off across the gravelled yard, biting his bottom lip hard.

It would give him satisfaction to tear a few strips off Bicknell, a man who had treated him as an inferior in the years before his new-found prosperity.

But the man had rung a warning bell when he'd hinted at his new-found arrogance and corresponding receding popularity. He'd failed in one objective already this morning. But had another tough meeting to face and wondered whether it might prove prudent to stop trying to walk over people and maybe try talking his way around them instead.

The town appeared up ahead.

Mono sprawled across a flat, wide steppe, half-encircled by the Askew Hills to the north with the Dinosaur River looped lazily around its southern perimeter. With the mid-morning light spilling in over the plains and the trees and brush filled with whistling blackbirds and jays, there was a village atmosphere to the place this morning even though it was much larger than a village, and, despite various recent violent incidents that had shattered the peaceful atmosphere of which the townspeople had once been so proud, was still dignified and imposing.

The undertaker was feeling anything but peaceful as he trailed an ungreased wagon down Plains Street, then on past the railroad depot, making his way for the offices of the Mono *City Clarion*. Editor Tom Kade was a former friend in danger of becoming an ex-friend on account of the critical articles he was running in his newspaper, as well as the way he chose to interpret certain recent events to which the undertaker had been loosely connected.

He felt like busting Kade on the jaw; instead he would try and attempt to reason with the man. He found the editor in his office setting type for the paper's mid-week ads. Scrawny and ink-stained, Kade's welcome was warm enough, he supposed, although Priest still sensed a hint of unease. The bastard should be uneasy, he thought, having worded his account of the bloody Frog Hollow business to make it seem he'd had some involvement in it simply because two men on his pay-roll had been involved, one fatally.

It was the Frog Hollow shoot-up, involving two and possibly more employees of Priest Funerals along with several thus far unidentified strangers, which had first caused conservative Morro to step back and realize that things were on the change here, and hardly for the better.

But even prior to that fatal night there had been a growing feeling that all was not well in the county. There were unexplained incidents of violence, secrecy where all had seemed open before, rumors, whispers, strangers in town on undisclosed business – all noted and illuminated in the pages of the *City Clarion*.

Although the sheriff had fully investigated the shoot-out that had rocked the county on its heels, he was yet to come up with any concrete reason why some local men should get to tangling with a bunch of out-of-towners, with death resulting.

This left the door open to speculation and wild rumor which extended to rustling activities, gunrunning to the Indians and even dope-smuggling despite the fact that there was not a shred of evidence on the jailhouse books to substantiate any such charges.

Digger Lassen, shot dead that moony night, had been a familiar character about the bars and gambling joints, but boasted no real enemies that anyone was aware of. His employer, the undertaker, was at a total loss to explain how or why he'd met his violent end.

The outsiders involved had vanished following the clash and the Morro survivors' story was simply that they had encountered the party of strangers while out coon-hunting, an argument had broken out and the resulting gunplay left one Priest man dead and another wounded.

Editor Tom Kade kept speculating in print whether Wilson Priest might know more of the murky incident than he was saying.

Although feisty and gutsy, as frontier editors had to be, the newsman couldn't conceal his unease when he looked up from his grimy type stick to see this looming figure filling his doorway in expensively tailored riding-gear and slapping his leather-covered crop against the top of gleaming calf-boots.

'Be with you in a minute, Mr Priest,' he called to cover his nervousness. He held up his type stick. 'Deadlines you know, always deadlines.'

'We need to talk right now, Mr Kade,' Priest rapped, his words punctuated by the sharp slow rap of his bootheels as he came in to stand by the leather chair hard by the Albion press. The stink of printer's ink and stale pipe-smoke and musty newsprint made him grimace. Give him formaldehyde and dead bodies any day of the week. 'About your last issue – and your next. I'm sure you understand what I mean?'

'OK,' the editor capitulated, glancing at the wall clock as he lowered himself onto a low bench. 'I can give you ten minutes, but you could cut that down to one or two if you levelled with me, Mr Priest.'

'On what?'

Kade gestured. 'Everything I write about you. Your wealth, all your trips away when you used to be here fifty-two weeks of the year. About Digger getting killed the way he did, with Reagan shot up. And I suppose if you really wanted to square with me you might even go so far as to confirm or deny that you have what we might call a romantic liaison with one of the younger ladies of the town ... just to set the record straight, you understand?'

Priest bit his lip and composed himself. He'd known this would be tough but it was proving even more testing and offensive than he'd anticipated. He proceeded to defend himself on all levels, including any suggestion of infidelity, surely as foul an allegation as any respectable married man could be subjected to. Kade asked questions but gave no indication if he was being convinced. As a newshound he was instinctively suspicious of the undertaker's remarkable change in fortunes. Wilson Priest was no longer the solemn and modest Morro businessman he had been. He now ate off Doulton plate and drank blended whiskey from a crystal glass. Two years earlier he'd been unable to make the council, now he was number one in line for the mayoralty.

So the man kept probing until Priest eventually lost his temper. He cast doubts on Kade's integrity and impartiality, even slipped in vague threats about withdrawing his considerable advertising account if the editor didn't change his attitudes.

He should have known better than to get into an argument with a wordsmith.

'Mr Priest, a man in your position has an obligation to the people, just like a doctor or a preacher, and fellows like you should never try and unduly pressure the press. For what would any town be without an honest newspaper? Blind, blinkered, deaf and dumb. Back in the Dark Ages, with despots, feudal barons and ignorance. Who's to speak up with the truth if not men like myself? And you should support us to the hilt, as you well know in your heart, Mr Priest – sir.'

Priest left.

Two errands this morning and both failures. It was fortunate, so he told himself as he climbed astride his glistening black, that such outcomes were quite uncommon. Mostly he came out on top, was quite sure he would do so in both matters eventually even if they took a little longer to resolve than he might have wished.

Almost noon.

There was heavy wagon traffic across the rumbling wooden bridge, which along with the new railroad bridge connected East Morro to West. To the right, halfway down Blackwood Street stood the impressive courthouse and council-chamber building, with its stars and stripes rippling in the wind, the copper-sheathed courthouse cupola raised like a gleaming dragon's head.

Visiting soldiers from distant Fort Hood walked the streets or stood on the corners. There were more women in Morro than in most comparable Western towns, garishly colored women of the night outnumbered by well-dressed ladies, cowboys and laborers roughly matched in numbers by men in store suits.

His town.

The thought always boosted him, and Wilson Priest was consciously thrusting petty setbacks from his mind and concentrating on the positive progress in his life as he rode down Blackwood Street and swung into shadowed Keller where his newly renovated headquarters stood.

Straight-away he sighted the young and limber-looking stranger leaning against the parlor's façade smoking a cigarette and tapping his knee with a piece of rolled-up paper. As the undertaker drew closer he realized that the paper in his hand was the 'strong man wanted' sign he'd had tacked to his front door. He reined in and looked the man over as he glanced his way. A snappier dresser than he'd expected, but otherwise strong and confident-looking with big hands and a sixgun on the hip. He had a hunch he'd found his gravedigger at last.

He removed his jacket first, then the vest and last of all his shirt. He was still sweating even though the day was chill and blustery with a knife-edged wind snaking down from the Askew Hills whipping up dead grass and gritty dust between the tombstones.

Thwunk!

His pick bit into the hard clay at his feet and he amused himself by imagining it was Chisum's head he was clobbering. But he did so without malice. Chisum had fore-warned him that cover in Morro would be that of a gravedigger-cum-funeral-parlor-handyman, which was exactly what he'd been as of yesterday.

He would learn on the job, so Priest had told him. He already knew how to dig holes, so he figured he was ahead of the game at this point. Preparing corpses for burial and comforting weeping bereaved were, he would concede, skills he would need to brush up on some.

It was quite a time since he'd worked with his hands, yet he was surprised to realize just how good it felt. There was something

49

about oozing honest sweat that made a man feel close to the land and distanced from the often nerve-racking and most always uncertain profession of the range detective.

But he was here to exercise both muscles and brain, he reminded himself. The reason he was here a hundred miles from Warrior Creek, digging a six-by-six-by-four in the unforgiving clay of Morro County, was not because he was eager to tune up physically but rather because Murch Chisum believed this regular-looking town by Dragoon River might prove to be the center of a major counterfeit operation.

He paused to gaze about with just head, chest and shoulders showing above the rim of the hole. A train from Dodge City was snorting into the depot in the distance, leaving a vast dark smudge across the sullen sky. At first glance Morro looked like any other regular cattle, timber and railroad town and he was yet to encounter anything that might indicate otherwise. Yet Chisum had seemed pretty secure in his conviction that information and evidence, although admittedly light on detail, indicated a definite linkage between Morro and the outbreak of counterfeiting on the wide Kansas plains. For the time being that had to be good enough for Chad Brodie to ply his new trade and keep eyes and ears sharp.

He was about to return to work when his gaze fell on the comparatively recent grave, four plots along.

He frowned.

He'd checked out the marker board which read:

Van Lassen
1850-1876
Murdered by unknown
R.I.P.

Convenient?

He was startled by the way that word popped into his head, frowned and asked himself why. It didn't take much figuring. Directly after Chisum's investigations on behalf of the Treasury Department had pin-pointed Morro as the likely center-point of the counterfeit distribution, further intense covert detective work had revealed that undertaker Priest and rancher Achilles had manifested remarkable changes of fortune in recent times.

This brought both under suspicion and, once hired, Brodie had been lined up to take an inside job with either man in order to establish where the new money came from, and if it might be linked with counterfeiting.

Then suddenly the undertaker's grave-digger gets shot dead by parties unknown and he had his job.

He frowned, shook his head and spat on his palms. The trouble with detectives was, some cynical sage had told him once, they could get so they suspected everybody.

At least the carpenter had died of natural causes and was to be laid to rest that afternoon. His first funeral. Priest had already given him some coaching in how he should look and act during the service. He should be sober and inconspicuous and wasn't to start dumping dirt in on the casket until the mourners had moved on. Priest seemed to take his work very seriously. So he should, Brodie mused. It had made him wealthy far beyond the level of most undertakers, and Chisum seemed sure the man was involved in something underhand even though he hadn't come up with any proof.

What Chisum had found here in his guise as an insurance assessor was mainly trouble, resulting in his ignominious retreat to Dodge with a bullet-creased shoulder following the still unexplained shoot-out at Frog Hollow. It appeared Agent Tuckel from

Treasury had decided at that point that Chisum's cover in Morro might no longer stand up, and so ordered another investigator be sent in.

He shrugged, blanked his mind and swung hard.

He had less than a foot to go when he sensed a presence. Straightening sharply, he stared up at the lean, dark-garbed figure of the sad-eyed man with a five-pointed star pinned to his leather vest.

Sheriff Cord McGee made it his business to run a check on anybody who lighted in his town for more than a day or two. He introduced himself gravely and hunkered down comfortably to ask Priest Funerals' new man a few questions about himself. Brodie obliged, peppering his responses with respectful 'sirs' and 'sheriffs', playing the ordinary workingman to the hilt.

'I expect you've already heard what happened your predecessor, Brodie? Shot to death in a fool gunfight. First such death we've had hereabouts in quite a spell and I'm not happy about it. Hope you're not the breed that likes to think he can solve his problems with a sixgun.'

'Not me, Sheriff.' Brad folded his arms and leaned on the spade handle, arm muscles rippling. 'I hear tell it was something of a mystery, that shoot-out?'

McGee looked away.

'I'm a man who hates mysteries as much as I hate gunplay,' he confided. 'But you hear right. That fracas up at Frog Hollow just didn't make sense, and when some survivors just vanished and others clammed up I was left holding the bag.'

The lawman paused to gaze down at him levelly again.

'But I'll get to the bottom of it in time. I always do. I'm not one of your slick-quick, two-gun badgetoters, gravedigger, but in the end I get the job done.' He rose to his feet. 'Like you'd better do here, huh? Pleased to make your acquaintance.'

'Same here,' Brodie called after him, thinking: an honest man? He hoped so.

Working undercover it was important he get a line on whom he could rely on and whom not, just in case Chisum left him dangling, which was always a possibility as prior experience had taught him. Chisum played to win, not win friends or fret too much about how winning was achieved.

It seemed a sad reflection on the profession he followed that about the only full-time professional investigator he knew of whom he could really trust, was Chad Brodie.

He bent to his work again as the weak sun broke at last through the low clouds.

CHAPTER 3

SONGBIRD

Brodie plied the broom to sweep up the crisp curls of yellow wood tumbling from the carpenter's plane as he worked on the lid for Granny Hatchett's casket. It was two days later and the parlor's new employee was settling into the routine.

Thus far he had done just what he was told, kept to himself nights and was careful not to appear nosy. But he was growing a little restless now. He was, after all, an investigator on assignment and Morro was his proving ground, the last chance as he saw it for Chad Brodie to show if he really had the stuff or whether he would wind up punching cows or pulling beer in a saloon.

He set the broom aside when the carpenter was through with the plane and had begun cutting dovetails in another slab of wood with maul and chisels.

'Best see to the horses, Brad,' the man said without looking up from his work. 'The boss likes 'em fed and watered on time.'

'Sure.' He hesitated, wondering if he should start in quizzing the graybeard on the goings-on at the parlor, thought better of it. It seemed to him that grieving widows could shuck their mourning black and gambol stark naked around the reception parlor and the old craftsman would still remain focused on his dovetails. He doubted he'd see or know much.

Outside the day was brisk and blustery again, biting cold in the shade with indicators that winter would soon be in full march across the prairie lands. He was tipping oats into a metal bin when Priest rolled up in his rosewood carriage. The undertaker had formerly occupied the plain framehouse beyond the stables, but not any longer. His ten-room mansion was about as far as he could get from the parlor and still remain within the town limits.

Priest stepped down and flicked his cape over one shoulder, dressed for traveling. As the driver waited, he strode across to the horseyard in blood-red boots, more like a man of affairs than a simple undertaker.

'Morning, Mr Priest.'

'I'll be absent for several days, Brodie. I trust you're sufficiently familiar with your duties now to know what's expected of you?'

'I guess so. Er, you taking a break?'

The man frowned distantly.

'Business.' He made a gesture. 'I'm not restricted to this limited landscape, fellow. I'm an investor as well as an undertaker but of course you wouldn't understand anything about that.' He turned for the parlor. 'Two to three days. I'll be expecting a good report on you upon my return.'

That night in his rented room – far more comfortable than his quarters at 32 Westbank – Brodie scrubbed up, shaved and donned a freshly laundered shirt. He picked up his gunrig with a thoughtful frown. A simple gravedigger would not have much need to wear a gun, he supposed, but an undercover investigator certainly did. In the end he put the Colt back in the drawer; if there was danger in Morro he doubted he had done anything to attract it as yet.

He sat down and penned a brief report to Chisum, currently holed up in the hotel at Milestone fifteen miles east in company with Treasury Agent Tuckel. *En route* to the stage depot to deposit the letter on the night stage, he passed the roomer where Chisum had lodged during his undercover time in Morro, looking for leads and keeping an eye on Priest and Achilles.

Chisum had found nothing to suggest either man's involvement in anything clandestine, prior to a lead that had prompted him and two other investigators to ride out to Frog Hollow on the tip that they might discover something there to their advantage. The result had been a deadly shoot-out in which Chisum himself was creased.

The whole incident seemed still to be clouded in mystery, but had been seen as both serious and encouraging enough by the investigators for them to focus all resources on Morro, eventually resulting in the hiring of Brodie.

Brodie knew that the person who'd slipped Murch Chisum the tip on Frog Hollow that bloody night was employed at Taggart's saloon.

The saloon stood off Blackwood Street on a lamplit square. It was large and prosperous-looking and eschewed lurid signs advertising beer and girls. The square was the place where young women liked to parade in the early evenings, even in the colder weather, and wherever you had young women there were always men standing about smoking, talking and watching.

One or two loungers nodded to Chad as he strolled by. If there were badmen and hard-cases in Morro he was having a hard time identifying them. Almost everyone he met appeared regular enough, and he considered himself a good judge of character. It was the bad who interested him, always had done. The bad, he hated. Growing up in a border town frequented by the scum of three terri-tories was where he'd developed his antipathy for crime and criminals which eventually led to his profession as an investigator.

Chad Brodie really yearned to clean up the West – and if he happened to make a name for himself and a big bundle of money in the process, so much the better.

He halted abruptly when he sighted the six cowboys lolling around the hitch rail dead ahead, staring his way. Suddenly Morro's night seemed far less friendly.

Flint tugged his cigar from his lips and angled a sideways glance at the stranger in the denim shirt. The ramrod of Diamond-back ranch, now one of the county's biggest since its recent acquisition of two neighboring outfits beyond the timber town of Deacon, was a heavy-bodied man of forty with hooded eyes and a twisted mouth, legacy of some past violence.

'Who?' he grunted as the stranger paused to take out his tobacco.

The runt's name was Willaway, the ramrod's gofer and one of Morro's least popular visitors. Some men were born to call the shots, like big Flint, others to trail at their heel like yapping lap-dogs; that was Willaway.

'New joker at Priest's, Flinty,' the runt chirped in his cricket-like voice.

'Kinda handy-lookin' geezer, huh?'

'He looks likely enough,' opined fair-headed Shields, hitching at his gunrig. 'Lassen's replacement, right?'

'Keerect.' Willaway was Diamondback's principal contact-man with Morro. Jorge Achilles and his hard-case range crew were infrequent visitors to the town, preferring to do their roistering at the northern village of Deacon which was closer to the spread even if it trailed far behind the bigger town in class and amenities. Willaway was often to be seen propping up a porch-upright on Black-wood Street in the middle of a working day, or loafing about at the depot watching the trains come in. Seemed his main job in life was to keep an eye on what went on in Morro; why, nobody seemed to have much idea. He glanced sideways at Flint. 'What do you make of this joker, big fella?'

'Let's find out.'

'Yeah,' Willaway said eagerly with a malicious grin.

'Let's do just that.' So saying, he swaggered clear of the bunch, hooked thumbs in his plaited belt and called: 'Hey, you. Yeah, the gravedigger. Who do you think you're staring at?'

Brodie flicked ash from his cigarette and came forward along the walk with hard eyes drilling at him.

'Didn't mean to stare,' he said deferentially. He tried a grin. 'Paying my first visit to the saloon yonder, and guess I'm not too sure how popular I might be. Nothing like working for an undertaker to ruin a man's social life, I always say.' He stopped and pushed his hat back from his face. 'Chad Brodie. I'm working for—'

'We all know who you work for, Brodie,' Flint cut in, raking him up and down. 'Let's see your mitts. Palms, that is.'

Brodie didn't hesitate, was suddenly grateful for the number of times, back in Warrior Peak, when hard times and dunning letters from his spooky landlords had driven him to take on a few days' hard labor at the tanning works on the edge of town. His hands were well calloused, a fact which seemed to please the Diamondback party; why, he could only speculate.

'Uh huh,' Flint nodded. 'You look the goods, I guess.' A pause, then: 'Where's your shooter?'

'Don't carry one,' he replied.

'Is that a mortal fact now?' Flint said coldly, coming erect and lightly tapping a fist into a palm.

The man indicated Brodie's midsection and when he glanced down he could see the darker outline of holster and gunbelt on that part of his pants which was normally protected from the sun.

'Usually, that is,' he added hastily. 'Sure, I've got a gun. Hasn't everybody? But what's this all about, boys?'

'What's it about?' Flint growled. 'It's about you lying, that's what. Now why should a new John start in lying unless he has something to hide? Can anyone riddle me that?'

'Hard to cotton to a man who starts in lying first time you meet him, Flinty,' chimed in the runt, striking an aggressive pose. 'Matter of fact that sort of thing can rile a man real easy ... don't you reckon, pards?'

Chad took a draw of his cigarette and flipped it into the square. Three fresh-faced country girls were promenading by. They seemed to sense the tension and hurried on. He was wishing he might do the same. He wasn't scared; had been round the traps far too long for that. He was peeved, however, but had to bite down on that as it would be out of character for Priest's new hand to start in roughhousing on the street.

'No call for anyone to get riled,' he said mildly, stepping down into the square. 'Not on such a pretty night.' He started to walk round the horses. 'Nice meeting you, gents.'

'You just hold up there now,' Flint warned, jumping down after him. 'You mightn't know it, gravedigger, but just a short spell back here some good men got shot up hereabouts, and one of those that done the shooting was a stranger to this town. We don't like strangers and we especially don't like cocky dudes like you what handle the truth careless–'

'Flinty!' Willaway's hiss was urgent.

The ramrod glanced round to see the badgeman standing across the square staring directly at them. Immediately the hardcase backed up a pace, leaving the way clear for Brodie to continue on his way. The sheriff nodded approvingly and strolled on several paces to join a small group of youngsters clustered round a bench.

'McGee!' Flint said venomously, spitting into the dirt. 'Don't he ever sleep anymore? Time was in this dump a man had some freedom, like the constitution says is his right. Nowadays whenever we show our faces you look around and there he is. What's going on?'

'Seems he's been thataway ever since Frog Holler,' speculated Shields, his face thrown into black hat-shadow by the overhead light. 'A guy gets killed and others shot up, and that tinstar still can't get to the bottom of it. Guess he'll be on the beat twenty-four hours a day until he does.'

The explanation made sense but Flint's mood didn't seem in any way improved.

'Let's go see Queenie,' he muttered.

'You feel like funnin' it with the girlies tonight then, do you, top?' chuckled pug-faced Connaught.

'You know I never pay for it,' Flint replied as he untied his cayuse. He tapped his shirt-pocket. 'Got a message here for the madam from the boss.'

They were sober at that. No Diamond-backer joked about Jorge Achilles and Madam Queenie. None dared.

Brodie entered the saloon and nodded approvingly. Taggart's had style. But of course Chisum wouldn't have frequented the place had it been otherwise. Even when operating under cover, he had to maintain his standards.

He shrugged the thought away. He didn't want to think about Murch Chisum. Or the Diamondback bunch for that matter. He wanted to keep his head clear and his eyes sharp. For this job might be his last chance. He had to nail it down tight. He drank two beers and invested a miserly dollar on the roulette wheel before the singer appeared on the small stage under a bright blue light to the accompaniment of a drumroll. The emcee announced 'Songbird Chloe' after Brodie had already figured it out for himself.

Chisum's description of this girl had been enthusiastic, and she lived up to it. She sang in a pure untrained voice, and if you didn't care for singing you could just watch her as she moved about the little stage in that low-cut red dress with blond hair piled high. As she approached the end of her number,

Brodie shoved away from the bar to make his way to the edge of the stage, where the blue light fell on him plainly. He applauded louder than anybody else and gave her his best smile and a wink of approval as the girl took her bows.

His success rate with women far exceeded that in his profession. He expected a response of some kind but a half-hour later with no sign of her appearing found him wondering if he might not have to try a little harder to get to meet 'Songbird Chloe'.

Then she appeared from a side entrance, dressed in street clothes now and hurrying by the crowded tables and the reaching hands. She was all sensuality yet with a ladylike style, so Brodie assessed as he downed his glass and moved in.

The bearded miner only grabbed out at her in an affectionate way, but suddenly he found iron fingers digging into his arm and twisting it downwards.

'That's no way to treat a lady, pilgrim,' Brodie said toughly, giving the arm an extra twist before loosing his grip. He turned to the startled singer and gave her the full candlepower of his smile for the second time that night. 'Sorry about that, Miss Chloe, but boys will be boys. Like me to

66

escort you to the batwings?'

'Well,' she said uncertainly, glancing back at the grimacing Cousin Jack. 'I don't know if that's really necess—'

'No trouble at all,' he assured, taking her casually by the elbow. 'All right, make way, boys, lady coming through.'

The mob parted. Chloe appeared impressed by his natural authority. Brodie smiled, but only with his lips, not his eyes. This was a serious business. Chloe Templeton was the woman who'd tipped Chisum off about mysterious events out at Frog Hollow which in turn had led to a killing, Chisum's wounding and Chad Brodie landing what could prove to be his biggest job ever.

It was a bitter night in Milestone and almost everyone was tucked away indoors as a sleety wind whistled down the rutted main stem sweeping it clean.

The solitary exception was the tall figure in the glistening black leather coat striding briskly towards the company store like it was a great night to be out and about, even if the sleet did continually put out his cigar.

Chisum took momentary shelter in a doorway to get the Cuban going again, then jammed it between big strong teeth and continued on his way.

The investigator in action was something to see. Back in Dodge City he might play the glad-hander and high-roller and be seen at all the bright places day and night for what appeared to be most of the time. That was because he had Chisum Enterprises running as efficiently as a piece of Swiss clockwork, so much so that it rarely required a great deal of his personal attention.

On assignment it was the opposite.

Chisum had risen to wealth and power by hard work, masterful skills and at times a scarely concealed ruthlessness. Right now, in this rough little nowhere town in lousy weather, he was working maybe harder than at any time in his career, for the stakes had never been higher nor the risks greater.

And nobody could even begin to guess exactly why Murch Chisum appeared to have made the Morro County counterfeiting case his personal obsession.

His contacts were waiting at the company store. They knew better than not to be on time, every time.

'Talk!' he snapped, making use of his pocket flint lighter again.

There were three of them, hard-bitten operators from Dodge in his employ who

68

knew what was expected of them and knew the penalty of failure.

As they delivered their report, some three doors along at Milestone's only half-way decent hotel, Treasury Agent Tuckel and Lauren Chisum were sipping on their third pre-supper aperitif in the diner, the man frequently twisting around to stare at the doors.

'You're wasting your time and energy,' his companion drawled. 'He'll be here when it suits him, not one moment before.'

Tuckel managed a half-smile and tried not to ogle. The agent was unaccustomed to the company of beautiful women, and Lauren Chisum was nothing if not that. Raven-haired, slender as a dancer and with a worldly personality that fascinated this conservative government man, she would draw attention in Dodge City, and Milestone was a long way from that.

'You certainly are a very patient woman, Mrs Chisum.'

'Don't you believe it. I'm just the opposite of patient. But I learned a long time ago that when on assignment, Murchell has no sense of time or responsibility, only results. But here he is now.'

Chisum strode in, drawing the attention of

diners as he slipped out of his coat, handed it to a waiter then headed for the table – the best table, naturally. Milestone knew he was the renowned investigator from Dodge City but none knew what brought him here. Not even his lady wife knew that, although the Treasury agent with whom he was working certainly did.

Chisum's expression was blank as they ordered their meals and sipped red wine. The man was excited but nothing showed. Travel from here on such a night was impossible, but they would be on the trail when the bad weather lifted. For the moment he was the perfect host.

'Sorry I'm late, darling,' he said, showing big white teeth in a phoney smile. 'Tuckel didn't bore you too brutally, I trust?'

Tuckel flushed but Lauren Chisum just smiled.

'Gentlemen never bore me, darling, you should know that.'

Chisum's face hardened instantly.

'I am aware of that, my dear. And it's true, Tuckel. Gentlemen don't bother my lady wife. Matter of fact she likes all gentlemen of all shapes and sizes. Don't you, darling?'

Tuckel fidgeted uncomfortably but neither seemed to notice.

'If you didn't want me to notice any nice gentlemen, darling,' she said, 'why were you so opposed to my joining you this trip?'

'It might be that I felt you'd be safer in Dodge,' he snapped back. 'Ever think of that?'

'Or could it be Chad?' she retorted, causing Tuckel's brows to lift. He hadn't known Lauren knew of their inside man in Morro. Her mocking smile flashed again. 'You see, Mr Tuckel, my husband thinks I have affairs with everybody, even men ten years my junior, although I must say Chad Brodie seems far older in some ways...'

It proved to be one of Tuckel's longest and most difficult evenings which didn't look like ending until Lauren suddenly appeared to weary of the verbal duelling and took herself upstairs to bed.

He expected Chisum to remain testy and angry, was surprised when the big man immediately leaned back in his chair with a crooked smile and lifted his wine glass in a toast.

'Pay-dirt, Tuckel. We've flushed Reagan, would you believe?'

The Treasury man's eyes popped wide and he breathed: 'Reagan!'

The Treasury Department and later

Chisum Enterprises had had the name 'Joey Reagan' on their top list for over a month as the counterfeit operation swung into high gear, and with good reason.

Treasury's first awareness of counterfeiting in the area had been when some beautifully made forgeries of the Andrew Jackson ten-dollar bills began surfacing in Plains County several months earlier.

Alarm bells rang right from the outset, as the quality of the forgeries warned that the perpetrators were skilled artisans, the forgeries so good that only an expert could distinguish them from the real thing.

But they were floundering for some time until sufficient bad money turned up for them to be able to draw up maps and draw conclusions regarding distribution patterns.

After a time it was obvious that the epicenter of the outbreak was the large town of Morro, and from that point onwards the hunt had centered there.

But the criminals were crafty and after following many a red herring Treasury felt obliged to seek outside help in the form of Chisum Enterprises, the most successful detective agency in the region.

Chisum paid off in quick time when his field men came up with the name of Joey

Reagan, a counterfeiter from Nevada reported to be now living in the county. They'd gone after Joey Reagan like bloodhounds, only to meet weeks of ongoing frustration, and Chisum had mentally given up on this so-called lead weeks ago and indeed had almost forgotten about him until his operators made their startling report an hour earlier.

'I can't believe it!' Tuckel gasped excitedly. 'How? When?'

'All in good time, pilgrim.' Chisum grinned, biting off the tip of a fresh stogie. 'But trust me. We've found him, we've got him and that geezer is about to tell us everything we'll ever need to know about this operation including the most important piece of information there is – where the plates are and where the forgeries are being printed.'

'The plates...' the agent breathed. Then he frowned. 'But do you believe Reagan is skilled enough to have made them?'

'Maybe.'

Chisum's eyes were distant. In that moment of repose his profile reminded Tuckel of some kind of predator, considering the fate of its prey. He suppressed a shiver. Chisum was one of the most dynamic personalities he'd ever encountered, and he was certainly proving his abilities on this case. It was the man's intensity that troubled Tuckel. It was understandable that Chisum should be committed and involved, but at times he felt his whole future depending on getting his big hands on those elusive, brilliant plates.

Then Chisum's big grin appeared again and he was offering him a stogie from a chased-silver case, and not for the first time Agent Tuckel was chastising himself for his bad old habit of simply worrying too much. This could well be the dramatic finale to one of the most alarming cases Treasury had ever faced. Enjoy!

CHAPTER 4

CUTTING EDGE

Blood ran hot and crimson from the sudden gash in the counterfeiter's palm.

'Next cut, the fingers go, Joey,' promised Chisum. He raised the reddened knife point to the bound man's eye level. 'No fingers means no more plate-making, thief. Ever.

You'll end up a nothing, too crippled to thieve, too bone-lazy to work. You'll finish up starving in some gutter like the crooked trash you are. So what's it to be? You either give me what I want to know about this queer money or you give up your fingers.'

'Please, Mr Chisum,' gasped the counterfeiter. 'I ain't made no plates or even seen any funny money in over a year now. And just look at them notes you been showin' me. Anyone who knows my work knows, like you do, I ain't never reached that standard. That geezer that turned out that bill you showed me's a genius. Ask your pal, the Fed out there. He's the expert. He knows.'

Standing shadowy in the doorway of the remote line-rider's shack on the forest edge, Tuckel quickly ducked back out of sight, a thin curse stirring his moustache.

Damn Chisum! He'd promised him the interrogation would not involve Treasury. Had he thought otherwise he would not have assisted in using his people to help net Joey Reagan and bring him here in the first place, even if the Morro County investigation had been dragging behind schedule.

He heard the ugly impact of fist meeting flesh followed by the counterfeiter's groan. Tuckel's stomach felt queasy as he headed for the back porch. The Federal man was a dapper, clean-cut and highly professional agent who could organize or sanction all manner of mayhem, yet had no stomach for the rough stuff when it was close-up and personal.

He supposed he had to admire the total dedication Chisum had brought into their hunt for the counterfeiter or his plates. He would even concede that one of the principal reasons he'd enlisted the investigator's assistance had been his reputation as the kind who got things done any which way without getting sidetracked by ethics, niceties or too much concern for his fellow man. The theory behind roping in Joey Reagan was sound. Treasury had collected any amount of the forged money in recent months but without a whisper of the identity of the all important plate-maker.

Best-practice procedure in such cases was to identify the maker of the plates and follow that through to whether he was also circulating the funny money or, as was more common, had assigned henchmen to do it for him.

Far too much phoney money leaked into circulation for any Treasury agent to sleep well nights these days. Sending first Chisum and eventually young Brodie into Morro under cover had been Tuckel's idea, and although Chisum had run into serious trouble here earlier, he felt young Brodie was doing very well at the moment.

But Chisum was a real hound-dog who wanted to get his teeth into the opossum just as fast as he could, ring up another triumph and get to pocket his sizable fee – hence unlucky Joey Reagan.

It had been Chisum who had traced some counterfeit uncovered in Morro City to loner Joey Reagan. From checks made by the investigator's own people and by Treasury, it was revealed that Reagan had had some shadowy association with another counterfeit episode in the territory several years earlier.

That had been enough for Chisum who was now totally convinced Reagan could finger his associates behind the Morro County ten-dollar queer bills, and so Tuckel felt he had no option but to support him.

But he didn't have to watch.

Tuckel leaned his hands on the porch railing listening to the night sounds from the piny woods. Bobcats and the odd cougar called this section of the high country home, but they were quiet tonight. With one ear cocked to what was taking place inside and the other to the night, the agent soon felt calmer, his stomach pleasantly quieter.

Suddenly three golden deer stepped silently into sight fifty yards upwind, a buck and two does. He smiled involuntarily at the dainty way they stepped across the faint game trail, was feeling almost like a man at one with nature when a gurgling scream ripped through the shack, turning his bowels to water. Thirty feet distant, a man was dying with a hideous rent down the side of his throat and his blood spurting like a fountain.

It was not Joey Reagan.

Chisum's assistant was a sadistic young man who, in between paring off small pieces of the counterfeiter's anatomy in an attempt to loosen his tongue, had eventually taken time out from terror to hone his big blade on a pocket whetstone while Reagan sweated. The blade was very thin and had been sharpened countless times to make its blade slender and hideously sharp. That knife was now in Reagan's hands, he having eventually loosened his bonds and suckered his tormentors in close before making his desperate grab for freedom.

Chisum's man was dying as he hit the floor and Joey Reagan, infinitely tougher than any engraving artist had a right to be, was coming at Chisum like a whirlwind, lips drawn back from bloodied teeth, the dripping blade reaching for him like a dragon's tooth.

Chisum drew his Smith & Wesson .38 fast and slick even as he went stumbling backwards over an upset chair. As he fell he fired upwards to hammer three crashing rounds into the counterfeiter's arching body.

By the time an ashen-faced Tuckel appeared in the doorway Joey Reagan was coughing his life away in a sea of blood and Chisum had the knife to his throat.

'We can save you, Reagan,' he lied, shouting as though afraid the man's senses might already be shutting down. 'A deal. Tell me the name I want and I'll stopper that bleeding fast. What have you got to lose now?'

Reagan looked up at the hard, handsome face and bought the bill of goods.

'OK, you win, Chisum, you piece of dirt. It was Hackman out of Wyoming made the plates you've been lookin' for...'

The man screamed as the knife sliced off his ear. Tuckel threw up and disappeared, hands clapped to his ears. It took Joey Reagan a long, hard time to die.

A half-hour later a column of flame rose

from the cabin, consuming the evidence of this night's dark work as two men rode away beneath the moving midnight skies. With two huge jolts of whiskey inside him now, Tuckel was feeling somewhat improved but still far from good.

'I can't say I wasn't warned about you, Chisum. They said there wasn't much distinction between you and the rogues you pursue for a living; I don't think there's any. Reagan was right, you are a piece of dirt–'

'Hackman.' Chisum grinned with fog breath coming from his mouth. 'That is Mr Tanner Hackman, Federal man. Tell me that's not what you wanted tonight. Tell me that name isn't worth a dozen Joey Reagans. Go ahead, say it.'

Tuckel compressed his lips and stared straight ahead.

'I'll have nightmares if I go back to the hotel alone, Chisum. You and Mrs Chisum can put me up at your rented house tonight.'

'That might not suit, Mr Tuckel–'

'It's not a request it's an order.'

Murch Chisum was a tough and dangerous man as had just been proved. But a Federal agent was a Federal agent. He only hoped his loving wife wasn't too drunk.

The dry creek bed wound its way down out of the hump-backed hills, twisting its way eastward to lose itself in the early morning mists still clinging to the snow-stippled Askew Hills. This was a lonesome corner of the county, squeezed in between the Dragoon River Plains to the south and lush Diamondback ranch to the northwest.

'How much further?' Brodie grunted.

'Only about a mile,' replied the parlor's yardman, a grizzled veteran of sixty hard winters. 'They've been prospecting up here for years, just the two of 'em. Old Mac'll be lucky to have enough to cover his partner's funeral costs.'

Brodie just shrugged. It was sobering work he was involved in but he was enjoying the cold morning and the big outdoors; not a whiff of formaldehyde anyplace.

The surviving prospector had his late partner's body neatly laid out ready for them. They loaded it into the cart and accepted an offer to break bread.

'He was a fine feller, old Rory,' insisted the wispish graybeard as he plonked refried beans before them on the cabin's tiny porch. 'Hard worker, saved his money, just no luck at all was his only problem.'

Sounded like someone he knew, mused Brodie, forking beans into his jaws. He frowned and shook his head. No. That was the old him putting his ten cents' worth in. That was all behind him. This was the Big Job and he felt he was making slow but steady progress. In fact he was feeling so good today he might even send a wire to his landlords when he got back to town; 'Rent enclosed. Under separate cover I send you a moose dick. P.S. I know where you live.' He grinned, but frowned somberly when the prospector glanced his way.

'How you like workin' for Wilson Priest, young feller?'

'Like it just fine.'

'Good boss, is he?'

'Good enough.'

'When he's there, don't you mean?'

Brodie glanced up. 'How's that?'

'I wanted him to come out personal to collect old Rory today, but natcherly he is off someplace, gaddin' and gettin' richer.' The man glanced at the yardman. 'Jest how does a man get so all-fired rich from plantin' folks anyway? Don't seem to make sense, does it?'

'Good beans,' the yardman replied.

Back on the trail and trying to dodge the chuckholes, Chad glanced back over his shoulder, then cocked an eyebrow at his companion.

'Got a point, hasn't he? About the boss, I mean. Sure, I know Mr Priest plays the markets and all that stuff, but that's a game for rich folks as I understand it. How do you reckon he got to be rich enough to get to play with the big boys in the first place?'

'She's really something, ain't she, boy?'

'What?'

The man winked at him.

'The songbird. I was playing checkers at the diner when you walked by with her last night. Bit of a fast worker, ain't you?'

Brodie was being given the fob-off. He supposed he expected it. Wilson Priest was a tough man to work for, and he sensed already that nobody at the parlor was interested in discussing him for fear of losing their jobs or commissions. He guided his horse round a big-boled tree and the cart clattered noisily over rough stones.

'I just walked her home is all,' he commented.

'Hard thing to get to do with Miss Templeton.'

'Why,' he grinned, 'have you tried?'

'Only in my dreams.' The oldster frowned. 'But mebbe I wouldn't make a habit of it, son. Walking that little gal home, that is.'

'Why not? Free country, isn't it?'

'Just a word of advice is all. I kinda like the cut of your rig and I wouldn't want to see you get yourself fired or mebbe busted up for no good reason.'

'How could that be? What a man does after hours has got nothing to do with his work.'

'Just a word of advice,' the yardman repeated. And the subject was not raised again during the ten-mile return to town. Yet during the course of that journey as the two men yarned casually under a sky dark with menacing cloud, he'd had confirmed by his companion something he'd heard elsewhere, namely that Wilson Priest was close pards with the boss of Diamondback ranch, Jorge Achilles.

Although cautious about discussing their employer the yardman did reveal the new information that Priest and Achilles had been young and poor together and now, reunited in Morro County, were middle-aged and rich.

He slotted the information away in the memory file he was compiling on the undertaker. There was still nothing concrete to link Priest with the counterfeiting operation, yet the more he learned and observed the more he tended to support Chisum's suspicions about the man. The funeral parlor had been doing just so-so for years, yet now was flush. The bogus notes were being widely circulated; Priest was absent from Morro frequently. Now that he realized that Priest had close connections with Diamondback, it raised puzzling questions in respect of the information he'd gathered concerning the bunch which had braced him on the square last night. Turned out they were riders off the Diamondback, Achilles' big outfit. He'd learned that Achilles had expanded his ranch crew over the past year, not so much with cowboys as hardcases of the Flint and Willaway stamp.

It occurred to him that if Priest and Achilles were involved in criminal activities, they might well behave pretty much the way they were doing right now. Keeping close company. Shutting other folks out. Showing overt and unexplained signs of prosperity. It was something to think on and no mistake.

He was feeling good by the time they got back, soon found an excuse to take a break from the parlor to go send off another letter to Chisum in Milestone, bringing him up to date on developments.

He was emerging from the post office when he encountered Sheriff McGee. He gave the lawman an easy howdy, but McGee replied with the fish eye and went inside without a word.

'Must have something on his liver today,' he commented to a porch loafer whittling pinewood nearby.

'Moody feller, the sheriff,' the towner responded. 'Reads and thinks too much for a badgeman, some say. And of course he's got a lot on his plate these days. That unsolved killing a spell back. Just like the killing of the man whose job you filled, as a matter of fact. Van Lassen. Guess it must be catching. Wire come in this morning that two fellers were burned to death in a cabin over Milestone way overnight. Things keep going this way, soon Morro County'll be as wild as the rest of the Territory, seems to me.'

Brodie took his thoughts for a walk. Two dead at Milestone. He massaged the back of his neck uneasily. Back in Warrior Creek he'd had serious reservations about going to work for Chisum again, for trade, but behind that polished façade he knew the investigator to be one of the hardest characters he'd ever met. There had always been rumors about Murch Chisum and his methods, and having worked for the man Brodie knew deep down that some of the stories might have substance. He paused to light up, dark brows knitted.

Once again, he found himself wondering why Chisum had singled him out for this job.

Sure, he knew the man had a high opinion of his abilities. But there had to be more to it than that. For he and his one-time employer and tutor had parted on bad terms in Dodge City. Real bad. Chisum's flamboyant wife had taken a shine to a younger Brodie on sight and didn't bother hiding it even after they were married. He'd been too smart to respond, but the damage was done when Chisum convinced himself they were having an affair and his dismissal followed soon after.

Strange man, Murch Chisum. Successful but dangerous. In the end, Brodie hadn't been sorry to go.

He half-grinned. Now he was back working for the man. Or working for the Chisum dollar, to be truthful.

He stopped thinking business as his steps had led him along the quiet, tree-lined street he'd walked last night. The Oak Street Hotel was small with a gable roof, an ideal refuge for a woman who made her living singing in rowdy saloons.

He was just in time. Chloe was emerging from the hotel just as he arrived, pretty as a straight flush of hearts in muslin and lace. He'd been surprised last night when she had accepted his offer to treat her to lunch, was doubly grateful now that she had. Chloe Templeton knew things he might need to know, as she had proved when she gave Chisum that tip about Frog Hollow. It figured a pretty woman like her would have a wide circle of acquaintances and pick up some interesting snippets along the way.

But who was he trying to kid anyway? He'd set up the date because he liked her style; it wasn't much more complicated than that. He sensed she was like him, eager to acquit herself in her profession and none too happy about having to sing songs for drunks and brawlers in saloons. Maybe Morro would be the making of both of them. Who could tell?

He was amazed how quickly and pleasantly an hour could pass. They were still lingering over coffee when the town hall clock chimed the hour, and it was over. There was another grave to be dug, and the earth of Morro's cemetery hill was hard and unyielding, so it was time to say goodbye, for the present.

He was putting the finishing touches to his neat rectangle in the ground four hours later when he glimpsed Priest's rosewood coach roiling in across the bridge over Dragoon River.

It didn't get busy at the bordello until midnight when seven horsemen from Diamondback ranch came churning down Star Street on lathered horses and tumbled out of their saddles at Queenie's hitch rack.

The girls were ready.

Although most of the hands were regulars, the cattle boss only showed about once a month to get his ashes hauled, and it was always a big event. At 300 pounds in weight and as robust as a bull buffalo, Jorge Achilles liked his steaks thick and his sex on the boisterous side. Whenever Queenie received word that Achilles was on his way in, it was her cue to stock up on food and liquor and to trot out her prettiest and youngest girls.

The dignified madam with the high-swept raven hair and cantilevered bosom didn't like earthy, two-fisted Jorge Achilles. Few did. The rancher was arrogant, trigger-tempered and unpredictable. But he paid well and uncomplainingly, these days more so than ever. Stock markets and share prices were all a large mystery to Queenie, but if that was how Achilles was boosting his income along with Hudson Pike these days, then long live Wall Street.

Soon the piano was tinkling and there was much traffic from room to room on the first floor as light spilled out into the frosty night and hard players like Flint, Willaway and Shields seemed intent on drinking down the moon while bedsprings creaked violently overhead and Queenie's nervous doorman chain-smoked on the front porch.

Sometimes Diamondback overdid things when the big man came to town. Queenie's man had always been able to control things in the old days but was less sure of himself since Achilles started in hiring personnel who looked more at home swaggering down Blackwood sporting twin sixshooters than roping dogies on the wide ranges.

The doorman didn't spot the solitary figure watching the joint from the vacant lot opposite but Brodie had his eye on him. And on everything else that was going on. It was damned cold here underneath this applejack tree, but that was OK. This was his trade and currently it was keeping a bottle on his shelf and B.B.B. and Associates quiet.

He stretched and stifled a yawn as a woman screamed then laughed behind rosy red drapes on the first floor. He would not be here but for the ranch boss; he was curious about Achilles' hardcases but his interest was limited to that. The cattleman was tight with Priest. They were partners of some kind and whatever involved the man he'd come here to spy on commanded his attention.

It was two o'clock before seven well-liquored men came roaring into the street. Brodie peered through the applejack to watch outsized Achilles fill his saddle with effortless power. Girls waved and giggled from the windows and the doorman heaved a sigh of relief while Queenie tallied the take.

Brodie watched the party lope the length of the street, expecting them to swing onto the north trail for the Diamondback. Instead they cut left, heading deeper into town. Quitting his hide, he set out after them to sight eventually six figures and seven horses strung out along the front fence of his place of employment.

Lights showed from the parlor where Jorge Achilles and Wilson Priest were sharing a drink and some sober conversation – at 2.30 in the morning! He found a spot out of the

91

wind and settled down to wait some more. The cold was taking some of the exuberance out of Flint's party and occasionally a curse drifted along the street to reach Brodie's niche. He wanted a cigarette but knew he could do without. This was his job and he loved it; some people couldn't understand that.

It felt like he was wearing a light coating of frost by the time the cattleman eventually emerged. The two stood silhouetted against the doorway's rectangular square of yellow for a minute or two, then good-night and Diamondback was back in the saddle again.

This time it was the shortest route to the home trail. Chad yawned and stretched, waiting perfunctorily for Priest to close up shop and head off for his luxury bed in his splendid home on the opposite side of town. The light died and soon the clip-clopping of the horse sounded. Brodie scrunched low as the rider went by to take the first laneway left into Oak Street.

Frowning in puzzlement, he trailed his man, reaching Oak just in time to see the horse disappear down the side of the hotel. His gaze cut upwards. A single light showed on the first floor, the room on the near corner.

It was Chloe Templeton's room.

Moving slowly along the opposite walk, Brodie stared up at the beige-colored drapes. A shadow fell across them. Another. The shadows came together. It seemed a long cold time on the street before that room was plunged into darkness.

CHAPTER 5

THE TIGHTENING NOOSE

The package from headquarters in Dodge City reached Milestone at midday and within the half-hour Federal Agent Tuckel and investigator Chisum were in animated conference in a ground-floor meeting-room of the former's hotel. The Files and Records Department had been working overtime ever since being alerted by Agent Tuckel to examine the records on one Tanner Hackman, the one-time forger of illicit engraving plates known to Treasury to have been responsible for the matchless quality of the flood of spurious ten-dollar notes several years earlier up in the North-west.

The information they worked on while two hard-faced agents manned the door, proved to be sketchy. Last certain sighting: Winnemucca, Nevada, several years earlier. Latest rumored sighting: Casper, Wyoming, approximately twelve months ago.

Chisum and Tuckel traded looks. Wyoming was much closer to Kansas than Nevada. They read on.

Last information on Tanner Hackman indicated the forger was in poor health and possibly dying, and total absence of any news on the party in the past year seemed to suggest he might have already passed on.

Additional requested material enclosed.

They opened the manila envelope and several banknotes fluttered to the table. Even Chisum could not be sure the notes were forgeries, but Tuckel knew it after a close study. The accompanying letter established that the notes were examples of Hackman's workmanship when he was travelling up and down the West Coast and the North-west, leaving a paper-chase of counterfeit cash in his wake several years earlier.

Tuckel grabbed up a ten-dollar bill and studied it intently with a magnifying glass. The current queer money plague was largely in ten spots. After what seemed to

Chisum a long uncertain time, the Treasury's man lowered his implement and actually smiled.

'Perfect match. Both these notes were made by the same plates.'

Chisum slapped his knees and jumped to his feet.

'Then that proves our ends did justify the means after all.'

Tuckel's face clouded momentarily. He still had not recovered from the bloody incident in the cabin at Frog Hollow when everything had gone wrong, a man had died and they'd likely missed a golden opportunity to further their search for the counterfeiters. He now regarded Murch Chisum as little better than a criminal himself as a result of that night. Yet in light of the man's extracting the piece of vital information from the dying Joey Reagan on Hackman, he knew he could not afford to be too judgemental. Even after their success in placing Brodie in Priest's organization, the investigation had been dragging its heels. Not any longer. Either Hackman was still alive and reviving his counterfeiting career, or someone else had his impressive plates.

Tuckel rose to consult his wall map, employing a pinewood pointer to indicate the places where the counterfeits had shown up to this date. The towns concerned were outlined in red ink, the speck that was county capital Morro, in blue. Although some of the towns were as far as 200 miles from Morro, with several across borders, it only required a glance at the map to see that the trouble-spots completely encircled Morro.

It was the discovery of this pattern which had first led to the authorities' focusing on the town. Treasury's theory was that the counterfeiter was both smart and ultra cautious and was distributing his forgeries well away from home base to escape detection. Too well, most probably. Proportionately, Morro should have seen more forgeries than it had done. Maybe the perpetrators were too careful.

Chisum had visited Morro personally in search of substantiation of this theory, but had found very little until a Morro entertainer had dropped a piece of information which had led him to visit a place called Frog Hollow where he might 'find something to his advantage' regarding the forgeries. The information proved sound but dangerous. Almost as soon as he reached Frog Hollow Chisum became involved in a bloody gun battle with men from Priest Funerals and Diamondback ranch, resulting in his wounding and the death of grave-digger Lassen.

What Tuckel was pondering now was whether or not Hackman might be hiding in the region, or if he had visited recently.

They'd discussed this for some time until interrupted by the arrival of a letter on the midday stage. It was from Brodie, reporting he'd made contact with Chloe Templeton and was establishing a friendship with the woman who had been able to furnish Chisum his first big lead the previous month.

He'd paid big money for the tip – stunning Chloe rarely did anything for free.

Brodie's report went on to relate how he'd become aware of the close friendship between Priest and Jorge Achilles; he'd witnessed a meeting between the pair in the early hours of yesterday morning. The under-taker was just back from a three-day absence; Brodie didn't yet know where he'd been. There was clearly an 'association' between respectably married Priest and Chloe. He'd found more and more indications that the hitherto struggling Priest and Achilles had both begun displaying signs of widening affluence at about the same time, approximately eighteen months ago.

There was more, but these were the items the two men considered and discussed at some length.

'I must say your inside man is doing an excellent job of work,' Tuckel declared. 'Good recruiting there, Chisum.'

'He's just a bum as anyone can tell...' Chisum began, but suddenly broke off, brightening. 'Just a minute.' He picked up the Headquarters letter, scanned it again then set it down. 'Your people seemed pretty sure Hackman was on his last legs when last heard of...' he said as though thinking aloud. 'What if, and this is just a "what *if*"... if he died somewhere around Morro and Priest landed the job of burying him?'

The room grew quiet as they sat staring fixedly at one another, minds racing. They were grappling with a new possibility. What if, indeed. And taking Chisum's big guess to its natural conclusion – what if Hackman had died in possession of his plates, a prize beyond price for any criminal? What had become of them? Or might Murch Chisum and David Tuckel already be starting to guess?

'Hackman, plates, dying ... undertaker,' the Federal man said at last, enumerating on his fingers. He folded his arms and nodded at the other. 'I've heard lots of wilder possibilities in my time, acted on some of them—'

He broke off as raised voices sounded from the doorway. Both twisted to see a woman arguing with the Treasury officers. A tall and very striking woman with shoulder-length raven hair, dressed to the nines in the very latest fashion from the East.

'Murchell!' Lauren called imperiously, tossing her mane and adjusting her shoulder bag irritably. 'Will you kindly instruct these flunkeys to step aside. Honestly! Give some people an inch of authority...'

'Lauren,' Chisum growled, striding across the room. 'This is work, damnit. I thought you said you were going shopping.'

'I'm bored with shopping and I'm bored rigid with our accommodations and this seedy little tank town and ... oh, hello, David.'

'Damnit!' Chisum snapped, but Tuckel spoke over him.

'It's all right, Mr Chisum. I'm sure I can understand your wife's situation. Clancy, allow Mrs Chisum to enter. We're just about through here, anyway.'

Lauren Chisum strode into the room as if she owned it. It was the only way she knew, being young, glamorous, headstrong and married to money. Tuckel had been puzzled from the outset as to why Chisum had brought her with him, but would eventually find out.

Lauren had had several pink gins at the nearest saloon in the company of a goggle-eyed teamster boss and one of her husband's gofers. She circled the low table festooned with maps and documents, then removed her lace stole, which Tuckel was quick to take and place upon the hatrack.

'Well, what's the game today?' she asked mockingly. 'Chasing, hiding or checking out the staff to find out which one is the spy working for the secret undercover bureau whose chief is actually a woman in disguise who knows where the plans are hidden?'

She was mocking them.

Chisum's face was stiff with annoyance as he returned to the center of the room. Tuckel was fascinated. He'd never met anyone like them, handsome, aggressive, temperamental; he the ruthless investigator, she mercurial, abrasive and very attractive.

'We're making some progress in the Morro affair,' he said politely. No security risk here. Chisum had spoken openly about their activities in her presence before, although he hadn't mentioned any dead men in his hearing.

'Oh, I'm so pleased,' she replied drily. 'Does that mean we'll soon be able to return to Dodge, darling? I wish to God I'd never decided to come with you down here.'

Tuckel might have commented that she was supposed to have insisted on accompanying her husband, but wisely kept his silence. Sometimes he imagined they said and did things purely to aggravate one another.

'See how uncertain my husband looks of a sudden, Mr Tuckel.' She laughed. 'You're really very insecure for a successful man who scares the pants of killers and thieves, aren't you, darling?'

'How far from the truth can you get, my darling?' Chisum said icily. 'But as you say, Tuckel,' he added tightly, 'we're about all through.'

'We haven't agreed on what should be done yet, but I'm sure we're of one mind.'

'Maybe we could discuss this later?' suggested Chisum.

'I'm afraid it will have to be now,' Tuckel countered. He checked his watch. 'There's a westbound stage leaving in about an hour. I want a letter on it carrying Brodie's new instructions.'

'Oh, poor Chad,' Lauren said, seeming to sober as she lowered herself elegantly to a low leather chair. She took a packet of Turkish cigarettes from her shoulder bag. 'In there doing all the hard slogging work, as usual. And I'll wager you're underpaying him, Murchell, you always did, didn't you. Always doing what you can to keep him down.' She paused then added unpenitently: 'But then I suppose you had good reason.'

Chisum's scowl was a warning for her to be silent, but the pink gins were doing the work they were designed for.

Lauren snapped a flint to her cigarette, inhaled deeply, exhaled luxuriously. She was enjoying herself. She was not bored any longer.

'I can see your confusion, Mr Tuckel. The big story is nothing much really. Murchell and Chad Brodie both courted me in my younger, more immature days in Dodge City. It was such fun. But Murchell won out, of course. He always wins. And, of course, whenever their trails cross, Chad loses again. It's the same in Morro. Murchell got shot there so he decides to look up Chad and send him in to stop any more stray bullets that might be flying round. Isn't that so, darling? You just hate getting shot at, and

102

you always were a very mean winner, weren't you? I should know.'

'That does it,' Chisum said angrily. 'Come on, we're leaving. I mean now, Lauren.'

'If you insist.' Lauren rose and extended her hand to Tuckel. 'Join us for supper, won't you, David? Murchell will be in a foul mood for the rest of the day now. You and I can chat. We can chat about Morro if you like. You might be able to tell me the chances of Chad Brodie making it out of there alive.'

She was almost too much for the conservative Federal man. But he liked it. And in just a few minutes, with a few gins for fuel, she had revealed things about Chisum he hadn't known.

'I'm quite confident Brodie will be just fine, ma'am,' he replied. Then nodding to Chisum: 'I'll instruct Brodie to exhaust all avenues for anything he can find on one Tanner Hackman, possibly deceased. Pull out the stops – probe Priest's affairs deeper – whatever it takes, even if it's risky. You approve of that, I trust, Mr Chisum?'

Chisum just nodded and conducted his wife to the door. She walked marvellously well even when a little tanked. Chisum was scowling and gnawing his lower lip but

Tuckel could see today, as he had done previously, that this hard man was crazy about his glamorous wife. Who wouldn't be?

He was left wondering if Chisum had indeed posted former rival Brodie into the front line in Morro rather than risk danger himself again.

He sighed. It was a dirty business they were in. But it was also exciting, as both Brodie and Chisum could testify, which of course was why both were part of it.

He went to the desk to draft Brodie's letter.

The sheriff never drank.

Whenever he was weary or had the blues, or if some crafty cattle-rustler was perhaps making him look bad, Cord McGee's storm cellar was his refuge and his strength. Occasionally he might even sleep down here in the room he'd fixed up directly beneath his jailhouse which had served as a dungeon for outlaws in the bad old days, but spent most nights at his two-roomer on Upper Oak. Nobody knew about his out-back hidy-hole, and down there he had his quiet, his coffee and his books and they could get him through almost any night.

The sheriff was a great reader and

observer of men. There was passion behind the schooled lines of his face. He was good at his job but yearned to expand his life. Reading helped but the badgeman knew he needed something more to fill the lonely hours, had thought briefly he might have finally found it at last when Chloe came to town.

Cord McGee thought he was in love. They seemed to get on quite well together but he was continually being put off by the way men were drawn to her, and how she seemed to encourage some of them at times.

Seated in his comfortable chair ten feet directly below his scarred old office desk, book in his lap, he counted on his fingers; she saw Wilson Priest from time to time, he knew for certain; she'd been seen with Chisum when that high-stepper was in town; she took supper and went buggy-riding with himself, Cord McGee, on occasion. And now the gravedigger was getting to walk her home some nights.

It hurt like ground glass in his guts to think she might sleep with any of those admirers, although he had nagging suspicions about her and that uppity undertaker who seemed to be growing fuller of his own importance every day. McGee was a romantic whom many women found interesting, but he was only interested in Chloe Templeton.

Recently he'd taken the extreme step of inviting her down here into his secret place to show her how he lived amongst his fine books and paintings in the hope this would impress and make him appear more interesting in her eyes than just a salaried town lawman.

He thought she'd been impressed; he could not be sure. He knew he didn't regret revealing his secret to her. He'd asked her not to speak of his 'escape hatch' to anyone and as far as he knew she had kept her promise. Sometimes he sat here beneath his gentle light picturing her seated opposite with a volume of Tennyson or Milton on her lap, just the two of them with the world locked away.

He put thumb and forefinger to the corners of his eyes and forced himself to think straight. Forget day-dreaming. Was he really interested in the dancer or was she just a diversion from the things that really nagged him these long days and lonesome nights? Things like men getting shot dead and his failure to get to the bottom of what had really happened at Frog Hollow, and why.

Now the charred remains of two unidentified men had been found in a burnt-out cabin – just another mystery to add to the rest.

He cocked his head as he heard a heavy wagon rumble by the jailhouse, causing his lamp to flicker. His guilt was rising; it often did these days, even down here in his sanctuary. He was deeply suspicious of certain powerful men of the county, yet knew deep down that he was prepared to overlook such things as unexplained sudden wealth, sudden and strange behaviour – even killings – in order to maintain his relatively orderly life.

He shook his head. He was a good lawman and knew it. But just maybe he could and should be one hell of a lot better.

It had just gone two o'clock Sunday afternoon. Sand-fine sleet was peppering the east windows of the funeral parlor as bad weather blew in over the Askew Hills. The last mean spell before spring, so the yardman predicted, but the undertaker knew he was lying. It wasn't even Christmas with murderous weather ahead.

But today Wilson Priest couldn't care less about the weather apart from the fact that it kept preventing him from dropping off to sleep luxuriously in his snug private room at the parlor the way he liked to at times like this, regular as clockwork.

The once quiet and conservative undertaker now worked hard and played even harder. He was robust and healthy but was pushing fifty and burning the candle at both ends. The room in back of his office was small, quiet and comfortable, just table, chair, bureau and couch. Most days he caught up on his sleep here and nobody had to go quiet about the place because it was known the boss slept like a log. Today should have been perfect resting conditions with nobody about and nothing to disturb him but that low-slanting, mean-cutting sleet that kept hitting his window panes like somebody throwing sand.

Eventually he began to drift. His wife had driven him down and would call for him later in the surrey. He preferred to do his daytime resting here so she wouldn't realize just how late he sometimes burnt the midnight oil. They had a 'happy marriage'. He was discreet about his tom-catting around, a habit he'd only acquired since suddenly and unexpectedly coming into money.

He must have been on the verge of sleep

when he heard it. Nothing more than the softest metallic click coming from the direction of the office; it was the sort of noise you would not even hear on a working day, or if you did, would pay no attention to. But on a sleepy sleety Sunday with nobody about it was just enough to lodge in a man's drowsy brain, starting him to figure explanations, and when that failed, to get up and go take a look.

In stockinged feet he made no sound on the parlor's sober-patterned carpet. The office door stood slightly ajar. He peered in to see a lean figure leaning over the upright filing-cabinet with his back turned to him. His first thought was that they were being burgled. Then something familiar about the man's height and breadth of shoulder rang a bell and he stiffened.

It was Brodie.

Blood drained from his cheeks. Priest was angry and on the verge of making his presence known, but decided against it. There was surely something strange going on here. What interest could his gravedigger have in their files? Abruptly Brodie swung round as though hearing or sensing something. The undertaker ducked back out of sight, heart thumping. If likeable Brodie was something other than just a casual gravedigger-cum-handyman – which the scene he'd just witnessed strongly suggested might well be the case – then he could be anything. Danger even. Possibly law of some kind? Wilson Priest's conscience was anything but clear.

He heard steps, darted away.

Returning to his room, he waited nervously for a minute before the intruder quietly let himself out the side door. Hurrying into the office Priest counted down the drawers he'd memorized until reaching that marked H-I-J. He riffled through the cards. One, filed beneath the letter H, was just slightly askew. He pulled it out and one of the first names on page one was Hackman T. Right at that moment, Wilson Priest was suddenly more fully awake than ever he had been in his life.

Brodie said: 'What time does the eastbound leave tonight, friend?'

The dispatch clerk at the stage depot squinted at him from beneath his black-billed cap, sucking on ill-fitting dentures.

'Nine sharp. You got a piece of mail there, mister? You can leave it with me.'

'I might want to add something. I'll be back by nine.'

'Suit yourself.' The man drilled into a hairy ear with a wax match. 'Say, ain't you the lucky boyo I seen with the singer last night?'

Chad frowned absently. He had weighty matters on his mind.

'What...?' He concentrated and added: 'Yeah, that was me. So what?' He was also testy. Chisum and Tuckel were pressing him to force the pace of the investigation while at the same time locking him in on the understanding that he could not afford to make any errors. In his past, the odd crucial mistake and scads of bad luck had consistently undermined the career of Chad Brodie, investigator. Like bankrobber Hollister getting rubbed out by the hick sheriff in Hoganville, taking his ten grand secret to the grave with him, for instance.

He scared the clerk a little and he backed up.

'Nothin', young feller. Just wondered how you got to get close to Miss Chloe. I been tryin' to cozy up to her for weeks but she acts like I'm invisible.'

At first Brodie thought he was joking. A gray-headed bag of bones with bad breath and squint looking to spark a woman thirty years younger? Crazy! Then he saw the way the fellow looked, like an old hound waiting for a friendly pat or juicy bone, realized he was serious. He also realized that to many in this man's town beautiful Chloe seemed to be the unattainable ideal, although he hadn't found her exactly that way.

Detectives saw and sensed things others missed.

'It's not you, pops,' he consoled drily. 'You see, I'm stinking rich, and that's the secret. See you at nine.'

He downed a shot in a nearby bar where he opened his envelope and checked his report to Chisum again. They'd demanded something on Hackman and he'd got it for them. File facts: Died Morro last year from pneumonia complicated by emphysema. Burial handled by Priest Funerals. Cash or assets: nil.

He'd also reported on a ticket-stub he'd chanced upon when rifling the files. Priest's initials were scrawled upon it. It appeared the undertaker had attended a vaudeville show up in Westburg two days earlier. Chisum and Tuckel also wanted to know where the undertaker went on his frequent trips away from Morro and this was the first strong lead he'd been able to come up with, as Priest's destinations were top secret at the parlor.

Unease crept over him as he thought about his clandestine visit that afternoon. He'd been sure the place was deserted. But during his hasty minutes in the office he'd imagined he'd heard something, checked around a little but found nothing, with Priest's inner doors locked up tight. But later, watching the building, he'd seen Mrs Priest stop by to pick up her husband in the surrey. Priest had been there all along. He doubted the man had been aware of his presence, but then again how could he be sure?

He was heading back for the depot an hour later when he picked up a shadow. He ducked into a doorway and the parlor yardman came limping by, glancing this way and that. He yelped when Brodie emerged and grabbed him by the shoulder.

'Looking for me by any chance, pal?'

The yardman was startled but refused to concede he was trailing him. Brodie feared he might have been ordered to trail him by a suspicious Priest. He might have roughed the man up to make him talk, but couldn't afford to raise a ruckus. Besides, it was hurrying on for departure time.

'Time codgers your age were home in bed,' he growled, released his grip and made it to the depot with his letter with just a couple of minutes to spare. All going well, Chisum and Tuckel would be in receipt of his new information at Milestone by midnight.

It was edging towards midnight as Wilson Priest approached the rendezvous spot on the spread's southern graze in the company of the Diamondback nighthawk who'd met him at the gates.

The riders followed the headquarters trail as it led around a stately grove of Coulter pines to glimpse the ranch house ahead. Achilles like to brag that his Coulters had the biggest cones in the Territory. They matured to some ten inches long, and when fully opened to spread their seeds could be as wide as six inches. Priest couldn't care less. He wasn't here for the beauty of snowy midnight or majestic pines. This undertaker was wound up tighter than an eight-day clock. They dismounted and walked their mounts through the gateway to the log house. Achilles' abandoned first ranch house was still solid; six or seven rooms, good roof, barn and bunkhouse to one side and a big-pole corral on the other. Utilized now only occasionally by the nighthawks and line-riders, the building had satisfied the cattleman until he came into real money, a great deal of which was now invested in the mansion he'd built to the north.

The rancher and four men emerged to greet him. Priest scowled at sight of Flint and his henchmen. More and more since their partnership had flourished, Achilles was getting to act the role of the swaggering gang boss, always with a retinue in tow. Priest was more discreet and, of course, a good deal more secretive. A sober pillar of society had to be sly and underhand if he wished to maintain his status while indulging his weaknesses.

He had Achilles send the men out of earshot before apprising him of the reason he'd called the meeting. It was to do with matters back at the parlor and involved the name 'Hackman.'

Achilles instantly turned sober and almost deferential. For it was Hackman and his genius which had made the partners rich. It had also made them criminals. Before the undertaker was through talking an anxious Achilles began asking questions. The undertaker insisted on summarizing before answering.

'He was at the cabinets, there's no doubt he was checking Hackman's files and that can mean only one thing,' he said tensely. 'Big trouble. Either the gravedigger or whoever he's got to be working for is sniffing around us, and now they've found something. Brodie sent a letter off on the stage tonight; I had a man tag him. So now we've got to decide what's to be done, and quick.'

'Surely it's got to be plain as the nose on your face, man.'

Priest's eyes were rounded. 'You mean...?'

Achilles snapped his fingers.

'Smoke him. Whatever that pilgrim knows or thinks he knows will die with him. If he's in cahoots with anyone else, then you'll have time to conceal anything you've got on Hackman, and we can pull our horns in, say nothing and touch wood until it all blows over.'

Priest looked relieved.

'I suppose you're right.' He clenched a fist. 'That upstart! I gave him a job and he repays me by spying on me and sparking my girl!'

'That's just your vanity talking, Priest. This is business.' Achilles beckoned him closer and lowered his tone. 'This is how we'll go about getting rid of that nosy gravedigger...'

'Yes, sir, madam?' Brodie greeted from the front desk as the couple from the hills warily entered the polished parlor, leaving the life and noise of the street behind. 'How can we help you?'

He was learning well. Always serious but never surly. Friendly, but don't overdo it. But sympathy by the dray-load was never inappropriate. Make sure the fingernails were clean before doing a stint indoors to relieve Margot when she went to lunch. Never mention the words death or dead, and 'croaked' was right out.

'Go on,' the woman said to the man. She was wrinkled as a prune but bossy, you could tell.

He flinched. 'You do it. It was all your idea anyway.'

'What idea would that be?' Brodie enquired. 'Or maybe I can help? Have you good people been bereaved?'

'Not yet,' he said.

'Soon will be, but,' she chimed in, 'the way he drinks he could go off any time, just like that.' She snapped dry fingers with a noise like a pistol shot. He flinched. Who wouldn't? All that rotgut.

'Hmm, I think I might understand,' said Brodie. 'You're planning ahead, right?'

117

'She's plannin',' grumbled the diminutive shrunken figure in sodbuster rig. 'Got her evil eye on the feller up the creek and can't wait for me to pop off so she can sell up and run off with her fancy man. Now she wants me to be fitted for a casket and pay for it so she won't be landed with the bill for putting me away. You married, sonny?'

'Not yet.'

'Want some advice?'

'How much will it cost?' she demanded stridently. 'Nothing fancy. Pineboard'll do just fine. And none of them big brass handles. Simple is as simple does, I always say.'

'If I gotta have anything it'll be cedar or teak.'

'You'll take what I can afford, bucko.'

'You just said I'm paying, now you're griping about the cost.'

'Just get on with it and–' the woman was seized by a violent coughing fit. Her faced turned blue and it seemed advisable to stand well back. She leaned against the desk and hacked and hacked until her husband spoke up.

'We'll take the plain pine, son, only make it for her. If I don't outlive her ten years I'll eat this hat.'

'Eat this, you old polecat,' the woman screeched and let fly with a right hook that might have hurried him onto the great beyond had it connected. It didn't. Fast-moving Chad made sure of that, jumping between them expertly and smoothly ushering them outside, all the while calmly insisting Priest Funerals would be only too pleased to meet their needs when and if there was a 'dear departed'.

The yard hand and secretary were chuckling when he returned, but Priest was sober as he entered by the side door in a hurry.

'Bad news from Diamondback, Brodie. Timbercutter's fallen to his death at Stone Bend. Wedged in the rocks. I told Achilles' man I'd sent out someone fit enough to help recover the body then bring it in. You're nominated. I'd like you to be on your way by noon. You know the drill now, take whatever you need. They'll be expecting you.'

'Sounds more than a one-man job, Mr Priest.'

'I can't spare any more.' Priest frowned. 'I've got men busy burying what's left of those two cinders they found in that cabin fire.' He paused. 'You're still here, mister. How so?'

Brodie left. There was only one boss at this

119

funeral parlor and he'd just spoken. It was ten miles to Diamondback as the crow flies, a little longer by the ranch trail. No matter how fast he was, he would be gone a considerable time. And with so much going on, this was not a good time for him to be away.

CHAPTER 6

DETOUR AT DEACON

It was a ragged kid playing hoop who first sighted the horseman riding down out of the timber towards the village mid-afternoon. The boy stopped and stared. Lying some fifteen miles north-west of Morro and several miles west of the Diamondback boundary, where the land rose in pine plateaux, Deacon was an isolated little sawmill town that saw few strangers. You didn't come here unless you had timber to buy or sell or were looking for trouble, and this straight-backed stranger didn't look like any sort of timberman to this stringbean kid.

He stood his ground until the rider came

in off the ridge. The light bouncing off snow was now full upon the man's face and to his young eyes he looked like something moulded from bronze. He toted a saddle rifle and a holstered .45. That was enough for the urchin, who took off and headed for home, bare legs flying. He vanished into the brush and re-emerged by the first shacks to holler a warning to the citizens of Deacon.

Brodie reined in close by the tiny frozen stream. He finished his smoke and flipped it into the water, to be swiftly borne away. He was tempted to produce the makings immediately and roll another. This was one edgy visitor come to the afternoon hills. Real edgy.

He looked Deacon over. An untidy scatter of mud-and-slab huts, general store, several saloons and one sprawling saw-mill where whirring disks of toothed steel ripped through former forest stalwarts as though they were butter, adding daily to the giant hills of snowcapped sawdust all over the town.

He glanced back the way he'd come. Had he followed the direct trail as instructed, he would be comfortably at Diamondback headquarters by this. Instead he'd covered roughly twice the distance to reach this crummy-like sawdust city tucked away in the jackpine hills. The reason? Simple. He had a hankering to stay alive.

Nothing about the accident at the ranch or Priest's haste rang true to him. He'd decided on that before clearing Morro, and this was his alternative route. He still intended making for Jorge Achilles' outfit on the river but he would select his own trail. Just in case.

Faces stared at him across a half-mile of snow-splotched grass and white-capped mountains of gray sawdust. He didn't trust small, isolated towns. The life made people suspicious of most critters on four legs and everything on two.

All he wanted here was information, not trouble.

He was careful to make no sudden moves as he eased himself out of his saddle and led the horse forward to drink. He leaned on its neck, outwardly relaxed. After some time his patience was rewarded when a man on a white-socked dun came riding out to draw up across the stream.

'Who be you, stranger?'

'Brodie from Priest's Funerals. Accident up on the big spread. On my way to collect the body.'

'You're ten miles off course.'

'So I figure. I'm new around here. But I still hanker to reach the headquarters by sundown. I'd take it kindly to come in and have you folks show me the best trail.'

'They're all rough from this side.'

'Rough doesn't bother me any.'

The fellow looked him over a little longer before he turned his horse, indicating for him to follow.

The villagers proved wary at first. They didn't know him, and he soon realized that they were not over friendly towards outsiders. But Brodie had a natural straight-cut way about him that made it easy for him to get along with folks when it suited him, and he was eager to hit it off with Deacon on a day that for him fairly reeked of danger.

Eventually Jackson, the bearded head man, offered him coffee and a pipe and he accepted this as evidence that he had passed some kind of test. Turned out all anyone here knew of him was that he was the new gravedigger and general hand at Priest Funerals. He let them know that it was in that capacity that he was making for Diamondback headquarters to accept delivery of a corpse.

His listeners appeared puzzled. They'd

heard of no trouble on the spread, certainly not a fatality.

Brodie nodded his curly head thoughtfully as he sampled his coffee, thick enough to float a horseshoe in it. Strong brew was just what was needed at the moment. Right from the get-go, this job of work hadn't seemed to ring true. Now Deacon's ignorance of any fatality up on the spread only seemed to lend weight to his unease and suspicions.

'So how come you're taking the long way round to Achilles' place, big feller?' The headman was showing curious also now.

He couldn't give the honest answer. How did he explain something as nebulous as a gut instinct that the regular direct trail might simply prove risky for him today?

'Well, to tell the truth I wanted to stop by here to meet you folks and ask about a few things that have been puzzling me,' he stated, which was at least a part-truth anyway. He'd planned right along to take advantage of his Diamondback chore maybe to rustle up some information that was hard to come by in town.

'Everyday stuff – such as how you folks here get along with Diamondback these days. I get the feeling in Morro that things have changed on the big spread recent, and not always for the better. Guess I'm curious about that.'

Although still a little wary, tall Jackson relaxed enough to concede that their former reasonable relations with their big neighbor had deteriorated markedly since Jorge Achilles 'struck the jackpot and started hiring the sort of fellers that don't rightly belong on any cow outfit,' as he put it.

'Men like Flint?' Chad asked sharply.

The man nodded his bearded head.

'Flint's roughcases along with a couple of dudes that look more like prison fodder than cowhands if you ask me.' He lit his pipe as he warmed to his subject. 'They come over the hills to do some drinking here from time to time, you see, so we get to see more of 'em than we rightly want. We're careful with them, not wanting any trouble, but we ain't comfortable, I can tell you. Just between you and me, Brodie, I'm blamed if I can figure why a big feller like Achilles would want that breed anywhere near his place nohow. Guess it's on account everything he touches seems to turn to gold these days. Could be the *dinero's* just gone to his head like it has your boss. Lots of questions without answers hereabouts these days, I guess. So what else was it you wanted to know?'

'The best route through the hills to head-quarters.'

'It's real rough country, young fella. Mebbe you'd best take one of the boys with you.'

'Er, I'm not sure about that,' said Brodie, draining his second mug of he-man joe. 'I just might run into a spot of trouble...'

'How come?' he was asked curiously. 'They're expecting you, ain't they?'

He was certain of that. It was the kind of welcome that might be awaiting him that disturbed him. Maybe he was being over-wary today, but any good investigator ignored his gut feelings at his peril. But considering Jackson's offer he realized he could really use a guide both to help him find his way through unfamiliar country, and maybe help him dodge any danger that might happen by.

'Sure they are,' he said, forcing a grin. 'And I'd be happy to have someone along with me. Much obliged for your hospitality.'

'I'll send Joe,' the headman said, indicating a rugged young timbercutter with shoulders like a working bullock. 'I mostly send my best boys if I've ever got cause to do business with Achilles.' His expression was sober again. 'Like I said, things ain't

126

what they used to be on that range.'

They'd already missed one stage to Morro and the next wasn't until the following morning. Chisum and Tuckel could have easily made the afternoon connection had not Tuckel insisted on awaiting responses to certain wires he'd dispatched after receiving Brodie's latest report from Morro. Chisum chafed at the delay. He regarded Brodie's discovery of evidence establishing that platemaker Hackman had died in Morro and been buried by Wilson Priest as virtual proof that their long-held suspicions concerning the undertaker were substantiated. But Tuckel was less impetuous and more thorough, which probably explained why he'd worked for the one employer for many years while Chisum wore fifty-dollar boots and worked wherever the money was highest.

Tuckel whiled away his waiting time in his converted office writing up the necessary reports while one of his junior officers hung about the rickety little telegraph station down by the abattoir.

Chisum was unsuited to the waiting game. He was testy and restless as he killed time at the bar across the road, where Tuckel and the delay were not the only factors abrading his nerves that long afternoon. The Chisums were in conflict. Again.

'Honestly!' Lauren sniffed, stirring her mint julep with languid elegance. It was an exclamation she resorted to often, particularly in a debate. And this debate was proving protracted and abrasive even by their turbulent standards. 'A person would imagine my only interest in insisting I accompany you to Morro was to look up Chad Brodie and rush him off to the nearest hayloft ... casting our garments adrift on the run, here, there and everywhere.'

It took a lot to unsettle Chisum but this statement coming from his own wife in the hearing of a clutch of wide-eyed yokels managed it.

'I'd make that my last if I were you, darling,' he said, putting an edge on the last word. 'You don't hold your liquor as well as you used to.'

Lauren deliberately raised her glass to red lips and took a long potent pull. Then she said quietly:

'I would back my ability to handle my liquor against your ability to control your jealousy any day ... darling.'

'God damnit all, woman! You know you insisted on taking this trip. It's got nothing to do with women or jealousy or...'

He broke off with a curse, straightened his shoulders. 'It's straight-out loco crazy you going to Morro with us. If our suspicions are sound we could be eating gunsmoke up there. Work, Lauren. You understand? This is work and you're acting like it's a social event.'

'I'm sure I don't know why you're still so jealous. I married you, not Chad, didn't I?' She gestured. 'Anyway, I'll be curious to see which way the feathers fly in Morro by the time you and your Treasury friend get through with the place.'

Chisum reddened angrily.

'Guard your tongue, damnit ... in front of these people!'

She slid off her stool to lean so gracefully and prettily against that scarred old bar that simple towners thought flash Chisum must have rocks in his head to want to wrangle with such a dreamboat of a woman.

'You're not concerned about that, Murchell. Besides, you're more than capable of handling anything that comes along. This is all about your lining up Brodie for a dangerous assignment down there, don't you understand? Your hiring him on the excuse your itsy-bitsy wound had put you out of action was so transparent. Certainly, you wanted a job done, and he was best qualified. But in the back of your scheming brain, darling, was the tiny little hope that perhaps something might happen to Chad in Morro, and then you wouldn't have to watch me twenty-four hours a day worrying I might run off with him. Tell me I'm wrong, sugar-baby.'

Chisum's face was a study. His wife was at once his obsession and his burden. He was crazy about her but not even he could tell if it was real devotion or something twisted. But it was true he'd had an ulterior motive in seeking out Chad Brodie and hiring him as his inside man in Morro. For he was still jealous of that man and had long harbored the suspicion that Lauren had married him solely because he could smoke dollar cigars while Brodie struggled to meet the rent.

Not for romance. Not for loyalty. Strictly for the cash.

He knew she would win this argument. She mostly won simply because he was so crazy about her she could lead him round like he was a stud bull with a big brass ring through his nose.

The big man's feet of clay were better concealed than most, but they were there.

It was a relief when Tuckel sent a man to fetch him. He found the Treasury agent excitedly clutching a telegraph slip and doing a little jig in the center of the room.

'From Westburg, Mr Chisum. In response to our communication the banks ran a check for counterfeit notes and the Garvey Bank turned up twenty spurious ten-dollar bills.'

'Tens!' Chisum said, starting to grin. 'We know Hackman specialized in ten-dollar plates. Tuckel, suddenly I'm about ten times surer we've flushed our forgers than I was when I walked in here. That undertaker's been taking the queer money away from Morro and exchanging it for the real thing, exactly as you speculated. Priest and Achilles are thick as molasses in the winter time – both of them are getting richer by the day – and at last we know how. We've nailed them!'

'Correction, Mr Chisum,' Tuckel said, sobering. 'It's one thing to identify the fish you're trolling for, it can be quite another to reel him in.'

'I'm ready to start reeling when you are. By glory, I believe we've earned a drink to celebrate this.'

'Couldn't agree more. And we shall have one. But if anyone deserves the full credit it's Brodie. His work has been quite out-standing. He's plainly an investigator *par excellence.*'

'He's a bum. Lucky perhaps, but still a bum.'

'We'll take the stage tonight and get there tomorrow. Is your wife accompanying you?'

'She says she is, so I expect that means she will.'

'It may not be wise, Mr Chisum. The danger, I mean. Priest and Achilles have shown themselves to be both clever and totally ruthless. Securing the proof we need against them may be perilous–'

He broke off abruptly as the other whipped out his white-handled .38 Special from its holster and slipped into a crouch, gunslinger style. He dry-snapped the trigger and laughed aloud at the agent's alarm as he straightened.

'Sure they're operators, Federal man. But so are we. And just remember. We know what they are up to but they don't know we know yet. That gives us a major advantage. With us two, your three men and Brodie, we'll stitch them up a treat. And never forget the wisdom of getting in first and hitting hard before the enemy even knows you're onto him. Could be in the long run that that might prove our best plan of action in Morro.'

Tuckel slumped a little. He was excited but nervous. He'd seen Chisum in action before today. He was in no way certain the man could be restrained when the chips were down.

Chisum smiled crookedly. He found Tuckel easy enough to read. He knew what he was thinking but didn't give a damn. He had learned early in his career that nobody really cared how you did the job providing you got it done. The ends justified the means, and if his means were often brutal and even illegal at times, they always paid him the money and patted him on the back afterwards. Chisum was determined to take command upon reaching Morro, then run this counterfeiting racket to ground fast and neat and beware anyone who got in his path. He would prove he was still top dog in his profession, and also prove to his lady wife one way or another that she really had made the correct choice in men, that she would see Brodie for what he was, a tough-enough nothing. But of course he would need Brodie to help wind up this ring. It was possible the man was better at handling the hard slog, the uncertainty and the high risk incumbent in a case like this than himself, he was prepared to admit. He only knew he was the better man by any standard and was always ready to prove it any time he felt he must. It just could be that Lauren might push him into doing that if she didn't watch her flirty step.

'You're not going out again, Wilson?' Mrs Priest demanded querulously. 'You've scarcely been home since your return, and supper will be ready in an hour.'

'Sorry, my dear,' said the undertaker, pecking her cheek then setting his best homburg on his carefully brushed hair. 'Business, business, business. So much has piled up while I was up north. I wouldn't wait up if I were you.'

'But–'

The woman's words were cut by the closing of the door, and soon rose the sounds of expensive rubber tires crunching immaculate gravel as the rosewood carriage carried Morro's most affluent citizen down the long slope leading to the town. Priest did have business to attend to but at least some of it was of a personal nature. In Chloe Templeton's comfortable hotel suite, he looped the fine gold chain about her slender neck, fastened it and kissed her cheek.

'Oh, Wilson, I've never seen anything so lovely. Where on earth did you get it?'

'Just a bauble, my dear.'

'It's solid gold, I can tell.'

His eyes twinkled with pleasure. A year ago, Wilson Priest, the sober, churchgoing town undertaker would never have dreamed of an affair. But that auspicious day when he had been handed the chore of collecting the corpse of a man who had died in a cheap back room of the Poison Pot saloon to discover astonishing proof of the plate-maker's art in the deceased's otherwise worthless belongings, everything had changed.

Even before the first counterfeit bills were printed and the first illicit dollar earned, the solemn undertaker was blossoming into the confident, arrogant personality he'd always been underneath the meek and mild persona he'd had to adopt as a lowly undertaker. He'd spent fifty years of his life with his sensible shoulder to the wheel, but from then on he'd made every hour count. He embraced gambling, fine clothes, a cellar of good wine. He hired tradesmen to build a great house and began dallying with the young girls at the bordello and other towns he visited and was solid ready for the big affair when the train brought Chloe to Morro.

He told himself he loved her but knew she did not really love him. He could live with that. Were she different, she might expect him to put his wife out to pasture and make an honest woman of her. He was as yet unable to convince himself that he loved her quite that much.

There had been one or two hitches in the relationship, the most notable being the time when she was also seeing that man Chisum, and had let it slip to the Dodge City snooper that he, Priest, would be involved in 'something strange' out at Frog Hollow on a certain night.

That involvement was to do with a transaction in gold with Jorge Achilles which was rudely interrupted when Chisum and two men showed, resulting in bloodshed and confusion.

But Chisum disappeared soon after that and Priest had forgiven her this indiscretion, just as he tolerated her 'friendships' with men like Sheriff McGee and now Chad Brodie. And she looked so good tonight that he invited her to accompany him round to the jailhouse both to discuss a couple of legal matters with the badge-man and to keep the social wheels greased.

Chloe agreed readily, for the truth of it was she held far stronger feelings for solitary, articulate Cord McGee than she ever would for the man who bought her solid-gold necklaces.

Chloe liked men and men adored her. It was the way of things and everyone seemed to accept it.

They found the sheriff lecturing an offender on the evils of stealing people's dogs, then returning them to the owners for the reward. He was surprised to see his visitors but quite pleased. He sent the dog-napper packing and organized coffee for three.

Priest's business matters were quickly dealt with, after which Chloe took over the conversation, always at her animated best with admiring males around. The sheriff hung on to her every word and Priest settled back on the jailhouse sofa and lighted up a cigar with the air of a man with all the time in the world on his hands. He was antici-pating news of trouble to reach town from Diamondback at any hour, was determined that when it came his alibi would be unchallengeable.

CHAPTER 7

DIAMONDBACK'S STING

Brodie's keen eye picked them out an hour before sunset, crouching figures amongst rocks and trees on either side of the ranch house trail in the shadow of a rearing pine-knoll. As the two watched in silence a sunbeam glanced off something metallic, and winked up at them where they sat lathered horses upon the high trail's last crooked bend.

'I don't figure,' was strapping Joe's reaction as he strained keen eyes to pick out details, faces, 'just what're them cowboys doing down there?'

'Makes you wonder, doesn't it?'

Something in Brodie's tone caused the Deacon man to stare at him sharply.

'Just a blamed minute,' he said, straightening in the saddle. He jerked a thumb over his shoulder. 'Back there a ways at the hickory stand when I showed you a quick way down to the graze and the house, you as

138

good as insisted we climb this here hill. Now I get it. You wanted to get up high here to see ... to see something just like we're seeing right now. That right, mister?'

There was nothing slick or quicksilver about Brogan now as he nodded his head. This was serious business.

'Sorry, Joe. You did a good job of guiding me through the hills. But you are right. I had a hunch there might just be a welcoming party waiting for me up here someplace, and now I'm looking right at it. How many do you count down there?'

'Six, mebbe seven. But what is the game, Brodie? You'd best tell me as I sure as shootin' don't like the smell of this set-up.'

'That makes two of us. Let's just say I had a hunch Diamondback might be planning to play some sneaky trick on me–'

'So you circled all the way round then came through Deacon just to sucker us into helping you?' the other demanded angrily.

'I figured if I just rode in here blind and not knowing the country, I could be a gone goose, son. Sure, I needed help. But I wasn't looking for a guide, if you'll remember. I'd have been satisfied just with directions. I wanted to sound you folks out about Diamondback and Achilles, and what you told me didn't make me feel any safer about coming in here. Even so, I still meant to do it on my lonesome. But when you offered to ride with me, I guess you just seemed so keen...'

'I was.' Joe's annoyance was subsiding as he stared down again. 'Truth to tell I've got no time for Diamondback nowadays. We were tolerable pards with the spread once, but shoot, ever since they got to hiring those gun-toughs and closed off their boundaries, things have sure changed. Truth of it was, when you showed up with your questions and all, I just felt I didn't want to see you run into trouble up here and ... hey, what's that flashing down there?'

Brodie frowned. The sun was at the right angle to glance off something glassy or metallic, which one of the party below held in his hand. The flashes were short, long, short, short, long again. He felt a sudden chill as he twisted in his saddle, eyes quick and darting, hand resting on gunbutt.

'Heliograph! They are signalling direct up to this here hill, which is the highest point about. And that can only mean one thing. They've got someone posted up here! You and me might might have just drawn the wrong rein, young Joe.'

Hardly were the words out of his mouth when the harsh, deep throated cough of a rifle sounded from someplace behind and above them where gnarled growth and clumps of grayish brush clothed the stony crest. A bullet droned close by and Brodie glimpsed a gush of gunsmoke and the momentary outline of a man's head and shoulders higher up.

That had been almost too close!

He assessed the situation in an instant. To cut back the way they had come would entail crossing that sniper's open field of fire over maybe one hundred yards. Suicidal. There was only one alternative, and that was to head downwards – down to where the ambushers were waiting.

The lesser of two evils? Only one way to find out.

As he swung, ready to shout, he saw that Joe was already heeling his mount down-trail, plainly having reached the same conclusion. Brodie's horse snorted with shock as he banged ribcage hard with heels to go rocketing after his partner with a great clatter of hoofs and traveling just as fast as was safe – plus maybe a little extra.

It was headlong, heart-stopping stuff, cutting down a steep and shaly trail plainly designed for nothing faster than a slow trot. A rifle spanged but the shot was high, indicating they had already cut themselves off the sniper's firing line in double quick time.

This left them free to concentrate on the horsemanship necessary both to keep in their saddles and stick to the faintly marked animal-pad trail as they cut lower to go sweeping around the first wide bend side by side.

For just a moment they had a clear glimpse of the granite shoulder below, where fast-moving figures were dashing across a boulder-littered slope making for the draw where their partially visible mounts were stashed.

Brodie's jaws muscles knotted.

Times like this there wasn't an easy-going bone in his body. Mostly he preferred to employ brains, skill and strategy to avoid gunplay in his often dangerous line of work. But at times like this when a man's life was plainly on the line for no good reason, when it was a naked option between standing up or going down, he could be as ruthless as the James gang having a bad day with the banks.

Right now he was ready to fight and kill, yet was still open to options if there were any. Now Joe seemed to be offering one such as he led the way to go storming below low-hanging trees then single-filed between solemn gray boulders which leaned towards one another over their heads like lovers.

'We can drop sharp into the canyon and follow it north a half-mile then cut back into the hills along a wolf track I know of which'll take us back to Deacon!' the man hollered, kicking into the lead again in a spray of dust and pebbles. 'We'll be long gone before those bastards know which way we went. It'll be rough ridin', but we can do it. Right?'

Brodie nodded.

It sounded simple.

But even before they had gained the canyon floor both realized nothing was simple in connection with what was unfolding here on Diamondback in the dangerous sundown hour.

Suddenly there was a second squad of grim-faced horsemen heading their way up canyon.

They had underestimated the enemy.

The pair had been scarcely out of sight before a fearful Jorge Achilles had convinced himself that his entire future might well hinge upon the elimination of one slick-smart hardcase, and he wasn't about to entrust such a vital job of work to half a dozen men when a dozen might handle it twice as effectively.

A side canyon loomed and shoulder to shoulder the racing riders veered into its welcoming maw, harsh hoof echoes hammering eardums as not one, but two hunting parties converging from opposite directions along the canyon floor rushed towards them, shouting and shooting like wild Indians to try and panic the quarry.

Brodie wasn't the panicking kind. A glance sideways reassured him that shaggy-haired young Joe wasn't either.

The open-ended canyon ultimately spat them out into a tight little gully with sloping walls, offering escape. But it was plain by this that Joe's claybank was favoring a forefoot, the limp more pronounced with every stride until the laboring animal abruptly went down on its jaw throwing the rider heavily.

Brodie sawed back on the reins, then cut his mount round in a tight semi-circle to come storming back. The manoeuvre was executed as quickly as man and horse could manage but still used up vital seconds. Crouched low in his saddle and intent on his downed partner, Brodie was still several yards short of his objective when the first Diamondback rider erupted from the canyon mouth a short distance away. He instantly identified the twisted face and dwarfish frame of Flint's lapdog sidekick, Willaway.

The runt was shooting and shooting straight.

Ignoring whistling slugs, Brodie leaned low from the saddle of his racing mount and was reaching for Joe's outstretched hand when he saw the bullet strike. A hit to the heart. With wide eyes locked with Brodie's, bushy-headed cowboy Joe felt his heart stop like a clock stopped on a dead-cold hour.

Raging, ice-locked with the shock of it, Brodie veered wildly away, his sixshooter leaping to trade hostile lead with Willaway as he used knees to steer the plunging horse for the sloping valley wall.

A slamming slug chewed up his pommel and he felt the heat of the near-miss against his thigh. Willaway was screaming excitedly and fanning his sixgun hammer almost like a pro, when Brodie got his range. His pistol recoil jolted his right arm and Willaway was punched out of his saddle to smack ground, jaws stretched wide in total agony. Yet somehow the runt kicked, rolled and came up on one knee to sweep his gun high.

But Brodie was closer by this. Pivoting in his saddle he aimed with deadly intent and got off a shot he first thought had missed.

To his amazement he saw the runt somehow make it to his feet. But the man was smiling weirdly through the gunsmoke, yellow eyes rolling bright and sick in their sockets. Blood squeezed through his frozen grin as a soft-nosed slug punched a crimson geyser from his bony chest. Crashing backwards, he vanished from sight behind a gopher hump.

Brodie leaned low over his horse's neck to go careening up the valley's low wall with spiteful lead either dropping short or ricocheting away on either side.

Willaway was dead but his henchmen were alive, shooting, and white-hot mad. Barely aware of his labored breathing, Brodie shot a glance back to calculate the strength of the combined parties.

He cursed. Looked like a whole damned ranch crew now! Until that moment the investigator hadn't realized just how effective had been the scare he'd thrown into Jorge Achilles, or how desperately the big rancher now wanted him dead.

His brain seemed strangely clear as he flogged the lathered cayuse over the snowy earth. He was interpreting Achilles' reaction to his visit as virtual proof of the 'business partners' guilt. It couldn't mean anything else. The undertaker and the cattleman linked together – in what? Crime? Murder? Counterfeiting...?

The latter was possible. But how possible was his hope of escape? This was all that counted right now.

He topped out the valley wall and careened away into sparse timber, but the hard-riding pursuit continued to push him close, with rifle fire occasionally ripping through the branches and bringing down showers of twigs and leaves. Abruptly, after covering maybe several hundred headlong yards, the timbered ground folded away downwards into an unexpected rocky basin studded with broken tree-trunks and crumbling formations of ancient stone scattered wide, a haunted piece of dead land in stark contrast with grazelands and woods.

Brodie jerked the horse hard to the right; intending to circle the basin in search of escape. He later remembered hearing the tell-tale boom of a buffalo gun but did not realize his horse was hit until it simply slewed sideways beneath him and took him into a slipping, sliding skid down and over the lip of a projecting slab of shelving stone. It was twenty feet straight down to impact point but felt more like forty.

Achilles shifted his weight in the saddle and leaked sweat.

Beyond the dead tree upthrusting from out the shadowy basin before him lay the dark searoll of the piny woods where hoof-raised dust was slowly settling now, the tender watercolors of the dying sun fading fast to tint the cattle king's heavy features with the hue of old lead.

Although given to violent rages, Jorge Achilles could be even more intimidating in his menacing silences. That was the case now as he stared down into the geological aberration known on the ranch as the Devil's Hole.

He could not believe it.

So seriously had he taken the previous night's urgent meeting with Wilson Priest at the old house – not a mile from where he now sat his huge dapple-gray percheron – that instead of simply delegating Flint's gun-toters to dry-gulching Brodie he'd supplied an additional backup bunch of hardcases just to make doubly certain the job was done.

Yet the outcome of all this stratagem was two men dead and two wounded, while Brodie was somewhere down there amongst the twisted lava rocks afoot, possibly injured by his fall, but almost certainly alive and armed!

He had to fight down his building rage; he sure as God made little apples wanted to cut loose. But self-control eventually prevailed and he forced himself to breathe deeply and slowly; he couldn't afford tantrums.

What Priest had reported last night had convinced him that Brodie had to be some kind of a spy who'd uncovered something vital at the parlor in connection with Tanner Hackman.

This was chilling stuff. For what did it matter if Brodie was just some lousy, low-rent snooper who couldn't even afford a half-way decent horse to ride? With that sort of information in his hands he could be as dangerous as a runaway freight train to the Achilles-Priest partnership.

He took another squint down into the silent shadows. It was a long drop. The bastard should be dead but instinct warned he might not be.

Achilles chewed on the bitter possibility that he'd made the bad hunter's worst mistake. He'd underestimated his quarry and overestimated his huntsmen. He turned to stare at the men unseeingly and the night seemed bitterly cold. In that ugly moment he was honest enough to admit he played a far better winner's role than potential loser in the high-danger stakes.

Then he reminded himself of just how high those stakes really were, what he was playing for, and felt his strength come back.

There was plainly no time to waste. That tricky gravedigging bastard had to be taken, and with night drawing on it must be done fast.

His voice boomed in the hush.

'Get the men down there, get him, and don't even think of reporting back to me until you can hand me his hat. Or maybe you find those orders too hard to follow?'

Even Flint, head honcho of the hardcase squad, was both impressed and intimidated by the boss man's simmering self-control, something he wasn't renowned for.

'Got you, Mr Achilles—'

'Don't talk about it, do it!' Achilles shouted, ash-gray features turning alarmingly crimson as the echoes of his voice reverberated in every rocky hollow of the Devil's Hole below.

The storm of applause washed over her like warm waves as she took her last bow before vanishing from the spotlight. Upon reaching her dressing-room door, Chloe found herself hardly surprised to find Sheriff Cord McGee waiting for her with a cigarette drooping from his lower lip, gray eyes appraising her as always.

She smiled.

A woman should probably expect just about anything on a night such as this, she was thinking as she opened the door and invited him in.

Earlier she had spent several hours at the law office with McGee, and had later witnessed the arrival of several grim-faced men from Deacon searching for one of their kin. Added to this, Chad Brodie had seemingly vanished. Then, while on her way to work, she had seen the lights of the funeral parlor burning bright, with horsemen in the yard whom she took to be Diamondbackers.

All very exciting and mysterious, and she was enjoying every moment of it. The saloon singer with the wide blue eyes and lissom dancer's body was theatrical through and through, a fact that her air of often tranquil serenity could sometimes belie. There was also a sense of melancholy and a taste for drama in her makeup which had led her to the stage. She relished flattery, attention, flirtations and having important people such as Wilson Priest and Cord McGee infatuated with her. Her craving for excitement had led her down some strange streets in her life but somehow lovely Chloe always managed to survive and come up smelling like roses.

'You can fix me a drink while I change, Marshal,' she dimpled, disappearing behind an ornate Chinese screen.

He liked it when she called him that. Made him seem something more than just an everyday town peace officer. The sheriff had his dreams but never let them interfere with his duties. His reading and study and foolishly trailing after a woman he knew he could never win were confined to his off-duty hours, and the sheriff had signed off duty tonight following the long and at times tedious visit by the undertaker earlier.

He fixed drinks and sat at the dressing-table surrounded by feminine things, perfumes, powder, frilly garments. Chloe looked at him coyly over the screen. Then she remembered, and sobered.

'Cord, have you seen Chad Brodie this evening? He's been gone all day, I'm told.'

'Guess not. Reckon I don't miss him much either.'

'Oh, honey, don't be like that. It's nothing serious with him and me.' The coy look was back. 'He just thinks I'm talented and pretty and wonderful company, is all.'

'And tell me, Chloe, just what does Mr Priest think about you?'

'I'm not sure I like the mood you're in tonight, Marshal McGee.' She pouted, emerging in a plain emerald dress with lace collar, crimson street shoes. She pirouetted. 'How do I look?'

That was just the trouble. To the eyes of a serious-minded bachelor lawman, she looked like an angel.

'You'll pass.'

She laughed and kissed him and he pulled her down onto his knee. Then he spoiled it all by saying:

'Mr Priest was sure chewing in his liver today, don't ask me why.' A pause. 'How much do you calculate that necklace is worth that undertaker gave you, Chloe?'

'A lot. Why?'

He rose, a lean-bodied man with an old-fashioned dignity.

'Lots of things happen in this town that I don't fully understand. You might call them mysteries. Priest's wealth is one, his and Achilles'.' A pause. 'Then, I sometimes get to thinking you might have some notion how he comes by all that money?'

'Now I get it,' she laughed. 'You're just interested in me because of the men I know. You'll be asking me what Chad Brodie's big secret is next.'

The lawman was sober.

'Not a bad notion, at that. You see, on top of other matters that have been much occupying my thoughts recently, I've got to tell you there's something about that feller that I find just doesn't quite figure. I sense there's more to him than meets the eye. I mean, just look at him. Smart, quick, a little too sure of himself mebbe, but a guy like that could sure do better than dig holes for a living.'

'Cord McGee, all I know is that Mr Priest is caring and rich, and Chad Brodie makes me laugh and has muscles. That's all I know or want to know.'

He took her by both hands.

'And what about Cord McGee? What do

154

you find amusing about that fuddy-duddy badgeman?'

Chloe tweaked his nose.

'What I find attractive about him is that he's always around and seems to understand that I'm always looking for something I might never find. Now, are you here to walk me home or interrogate me?'

They left hand in hand, strolling through the barroom, the sheriff the focus of many an envious eye. The crowd was light on numbers tonight, with nobody in from Diamondback as far as the sheriff could tell. He was considering inviting Chloe to the cellar for a platonic glass of wine as they approached the batwings, where both pulled up sharply as a man wearing sombrero and batwing chaps came shouldering through.

'Hey, Sheriff, just the man I'm lookin' for,' panted the Diamondback horse wrangler. He tugged off his hat and waved it about as he spoke. 'Mr Achilles sent me in to tell you the gravedigger killed a Deacon feller and one of our boys on the spread tonight, and that we think we might have him cornered at Devil's Hole. He don't need no help, says he can handle it hisself, just figgered you ought to know was all.'

Taggart's was hushed for a long moment

before Chloe Templeton broke the shocked silence.

'I don't believe it!' she cried.

Yet it seemed plain from the sudden clamor of voices that there appeared already to be plenty here who did.

The cowboy's sturdy legs were threshing, his spurs cutting white furrows in the dark stone as the steel arm across his windpipe grew tighter and tighter.

'Arrghh!' he gasped, and the arm around his throat snapped upwards sharply to catch him under the jaw and silence him. The man sagged dazedly and Brodie altered his grip, and slammed the top of his head into the dead tree trunk.

The man collapsed as though dead with one leg tucked beneath him, head at an ugly angle. Quickly Brodie straightened his body out then leaned his ear close to the gaping mouth.

Still breathing. This was one waddy's lucky night.

He grabbed up his gun and thrust it into his belt. They were still searching for him and this one had gotten too close. But the sounds of the struggle could have been overheard. He ghosted away, stockinged feet making no noise in the Devil's Hole.

Where was he headed now? he thought. He propped, head swiveling. The moon was east, and he was heading that way. But he wanted to go south. South lay Morro. He grimaced. Yeah, south – with five miles of rangeland and riverland in-between. But he had to have an objective. If he stayed in the basin long enough they would surely get him. Their numbers would make that inevitable.

As he moved there was the distant brush of his feet in dead leaves, the jarring sound of a searcher's sudden shout. Moonlight snowed everything and white stars blazed.

He paused before a pale rock formation shaped like a figure at prayer. He had a burning torch in each lung and blood from his hand dripped softly as he stood turning his head from side to side like a wild hunted creature, which he supposed was what he was.

Two men dead for certain. Maybe upwards of a dozen hands still combing the stone maze. The occasional bellow came from above.

Achilles' voice.

At one stage when it had seemed im-possible he would survive, he had briefly considered doubling back to the north side of the basin and making a try to take Achilles out of the game with a .45 bullet. Achilles was trying to murder him; Achilles and Priest – he was certain of it. That fat bastard deserved to die, but not as much as Chad Brodie believed he had a right to stay alive – and get to discover if the killers were also the counterfeiters.

Besides, he'd reminded himself, he was an investigator, not a killer. The decision he'd come to in the end – fight his way across the basin then hopefully escape it and vanish into the pines – was proving risky as hell but was so far successful.

He slipped between two scarred boulders into darkness. A massive overhang of stone shadowed him, ahead a column of moonlight probed a hole. He sensed he'd about reached the southern boundary of Diamondback ranch's rocky section of no-cows-to-the-acre terrain as he hauled himself upwards towards that single shaft of light.

His foot dislodged a pebble. Immediately a head appeared in the hole above, moonlight winking on gunmetal and falling on Brodie's upturned face. The man pointed a revolver at him as Brodie leapt high. His hand clutched an arm and the startled gunman emitted one sharp yip of surprise as he was dragged through the hole, his cry chopping off suddenly as his head struck rock.

Panting, air rasping in his lungs, Brodie released his grip. The unconscious form went sliding and slithering downslope into blackness, and he was crawling up through nature's manhole.

He could have killed the man but figured he'd done more than enough of that for one day. Maybe Chisum had calculated he was capable of killing if put to it when he'd hired him to take over for him in operation Morro.

He was out.

He ran fast across open ground. Soon he could hear them coming; they'd have to be blind not to spot him out here in the open.

A stand of pines showed ahead. He changed direction and headed for it. Tall dark trees loomed. He plunged in. The shadows were black as a batwing and he was a hunted animal eating up distance in huge leaping bounds, his mind blank now; hardluck Chad Brodie running for his life.

It was cold as a sea cave in the mid-winter woods but he was leaving a trail of sweat behind so that the huntsmen could easily have trailed him had they had dogs. But all they had were guns and horses and those weren't proving enough. Yet.

His rushing figure disturbed a big animal somewhere in the pine-scented gloom. The beast went crashing away to the west and the horsemen heard and followed it. Brodie was all alone by the time the timber thinned out, and he sped unhindered across acres of dreaming rangeland, scaring the cattle and drawing a string of critical hoots from a crotchety owl.

His smooth-running gait eventually disintegrated into a stagger and thirst was killing him by the time he limped across the ranch's borderline to glimpse the first lights, which he correctly guessed might be the undertaker's mansion on the hill.

He gave the place a wide berth, threading his way through orchards, cow yards, along back streets, keeping low and quiet.

One thing was plain. He must find a hideaway fast someplace in the town. If daybreak found him still in the open they would bring in the dogs and flush him out. With lights going on and the distant sound of horsemen, the town was coming awake, and you could guarantee it would be a tense and jittery town following the violent events on Diamondback.

He knew it was time to start figuring just

160

who might extend a desperate range detective a helping hand. It promised to be a short list.

CHAPTER 8

FUGITIVE WITH A GUN

Just on daybreak a rumbling juggernaut of thundercloud came breaking in over the Askew Hills to dump its burdensome deluge squarely upon the town. Rain hammered deafeningly upon tin rooftops, overflowed the rainspouts and gurgled in guttural undertones beneath the general store which had suddenly became the focal point for cursing and half-drowned searchers who suddenly came dashing for cover.

'So much for trackin' that bastard by daylight,' panted Flint, shaking water from his hat onto somebody's jacket.

'Anyways, at least we seen more'n enough by lamplight to be dead-set certain that tricky sonuva made it here, pardner,' consoled pale-eyed Shields, sleeving his mouth and reaching for his tobacco. 'And we're next door to sure he weren't able to get a hoss and get gone before the sheriff got the search organized.' The man broke off as a party of mackinawed horsemen appeared along the rain-lashed street. Peering through the downpour they were soon able to identify the slender upright figure of Sheriff McGee in the vanguard, trailed by amongst others, all looking miserable, Wilson Priest forking his handsome black. The lawman's face showed pale beneath his dripping hatbrim as he drew to a halt beyond the sluicing overhang.

'Any sign?'

He wasn't hopeful. He'd already figured they wouldn't be just standing about morosely if they'd bagged their man, would they? Heads shook in response and their silent stares were critical bordering on the downright suspicious. There had been a general feeling in Morro ever since the Frog Hollow affair that McGee hadn't pushed his enquiry as hard as he might have done, due to the possibility that men connected with both Priest and Achilles, the most powerful men in the county, had been involved. But the news of gun violence on Diamondback overnight had at last galvanized the lawman into action. The man was expected to show determination in running Brodie to earth in order to get his version of bloody events before angry avengers got in ahead of them and tried to lynch the man.

McGee wasn't surprised to learn that his quarry had been neither sighted nor heard of since the gunplay in the country. The longer this manhunt continued the tougher and more dangerous the gravedigger seemed to appear. The very fact that Brodie was alleged to have shot two men before giving the Diamondback's entire crew the slip to make it safely back to town, seemed like evidence enough that Priest Funerals' new hand simply had to be more than a simple gravedigger. Much more, if he was any guess.

McGee rode on, bawling orders. But Priest cut his black into the hitch rail and stiffly swung down. He'd sighted Achilles by the closed doors, and they had to talk. They needed to talk real bad.

The storekeeper was ordered, not asked, to provide space and privacy and keep everyone else out. Flint and Shields guarded the doors and windows throughout the conference which was brief and resulted in a unanimous decision. Brodie simply had to be found and silenced before he could reveal whatever he knew, or thought he knew, about the late Tanner Hackman. The conspirators had already combined to try and nail the gravedigger and had failed miserably. Now, like the sheriff, they were interpreting the manner in which Brodie had survived against heavy odds as evidence of the threat he posed.

And guilty men were now thinking: that tough bastard might even be some kind of law!

They were badly shaken, bordering on scared. There was no way they could not be. This was the first time in their criminal partnership they'd felt seriously threatened. Lady Luck had proved their friend over time but they were feeling a long way from her as they pondered the possibilities of failure.

But plainly there was but one single solution.

Brodie must go. Now.

But where could the tricky son of a bitch be holed up? They'd already combed the town end to end; it looked as though there was nothing for it but to begin again. The rainstorm was gone by now, the passing thunder fading far off into a rustling drum-beat out over the plains.

With sheriff, Priest and Achilles now sharing command, the search got under way again. As they had been doing all night, squads of men moved systematically from block to block with guns in hand, knocking on doors, searching beneath buildings, but seemingly only succeeding in once again disturbing spiders, pack-rats, chickens and several crotchety bums from the haylofts of Morro by the time the sun peered through a rent in the clouds and planks were laid across the muddy streets.

Everyone in town, so it seemed, was wet, weary, agitated and just a little afraid, whether they were searchers or onlookers. The bloodshed at Frog Hollow had first jolted this hitherto peaceful railroad town out of its complacency, while subsequent violence and gunshot deaths in the night had jarred its very foundations. Theories both logical and outrageous were advanced concerning just how and with whose assistance their quarry had obviously now found some kind of sanctuary.

It suited them to picture Brodie as exhausted and desperate in some leaking rat-hole, which they must uncover sooner or later. When in truth he was lolling back in an armchair sipping whiskey-laced coffee from a porcelain mug with a pretty woman gently soaking his blistered feet in a dish of steaming water. Much more than a simple gravedigger, for certain.

The town clock struck ten as the trail-spattered Concord coach wheeled into the stage depot adjacent to the railroad station, dead on time despite storms and flooded creeks and the delay caused by a teamer throwing a shoe. Ever since the railroad had brought in competition the stage company had become meticulous about punctuality and schedules. Which suited these new arrivals just fine; they hadn't been able to get here quick enough to suit them. But by the time their luggage had been toted inside and they'd shaken some of the travel kinks loose, Chisum and Tuckel sensed they should have reached town yesterday, maybe even earlier.

They'd come to confer with Brodie only to discover they might be last in a long queue of a citizens who also wanted to do just that.

Tuckel was gray around the gills by the time they'd checked into the hotel and sat down to a breakfast none of them really wanted. Boot-heels clumped on porch-boards outside. Someplace a man shouted, his voice engulfed by urgent hoofbeats. Chisum shrugged out of his greatcoat and poured himself a double slug from the bottle he'd ordered. Abstemious Tuckel joined him, but Chisum's annoyance was plain when his wife placed her hand over her glass.

'Not drinking, darling?' he said edgily. 'You drink at the drop of a hat. But now we've all got good reason to, you say no. Ever knew a man who could understand a woman's mind, Tuckel?'

'What's he done here?' Tuckel almost croaked, his Adam's apple bobbing. 'He must have gone berserk ... all this gunplay. I thought you assured me Brodie would prove the ideal man for our purposes here, Mr Chisum. Solid, reliable in a crisis, astute investigator. Damnation! He's a cowboy. He shoots people.'

'Please restrain yourself, Mr Tuckel,' chided a pale Lauren. 'What my husband said about Chad is all true. I think we'll find he was about Treasury business and something went amiss. Wouldn't you agree, Murchell?'

'What I'd agree to is that you'd support Brodie if he assassinated the President,' Chisum retorted sourly. But then he nodded.

'But I guess you're right. It only seems as though Brodie has run hog-wild. We know he went out to Achilles' spread yesterday, which makes it a certainty he was following up the connection between that rancher and Priest. What happened there we can't be sure. All we know is the result, and that's just about as bad as it could get.'

'Why do you say that?' Lauren's tone was challenging. It was true what her husband said. She always supported Chad Brodie.

Between slugs of rye and black coffee Chisum began summarising the situation aloud, as much to clarify his own thinking as to illuminate theirs.

'Brodie has fouled up.' His tone was uncompromising.

'Probably had the right intentions, but good intentions don't boil beans. We were ready to move in on Priest and Achilles quietly and smoothly, and, yeah, I still believe we'll find they're our counterfeiters. But Brodie's muddied the waters and thrown the whole damn operation into a spin, and it's gone way beyond the point where we could reveal he was working for Treasury, Tuckel. The government can't be connected to violence like this publicly and neither can I for that matter.'

The smooth, hard features were grim as he stared from one to the other. When he spoke his tone was low and chilling.

'We can't do a thing while Brodie's at large ... and we can't risk him going on trial and spilling everything if they catch him...'

'What in God's name are you saying, Murchell?' Lauren demanded, the color draining from her face as she rose. 'You sound as though you are washing your hands of him.'

The big man leaned back and spread his hands.

'I am saying the man is a liability. Stating the facts. Black and white, baby. Your old friend and mine has come up a loser again.'

'You're ready to throw him to the lions!' she accused, jumping to her feet. 'And why aren't I surprised? Why was it I had my suspicions about this whole affair of you hiring Chad again ... why I insisted on accompanying you south? It was so I could watch out for a man who is worth ten of you, my darling husband. I feared he would come to some harm, and how right I was. Well, I won't let you kill him – I won't! Believe that if you never believed anything else – baby!' She was gone in a flurry of skirts and a swish of long dark tresses.

Iron-jawed and bitter-eyed, Chisum nodded to himself as though in recognition of some secret inner truth.

Out on the street, a cart with muddy-booted men hanging off the sides, clutching guns, went rattling by. Across at the barber's, two big men in mackinaws stood together locked in earnest conversation. Achilles and Priest appeared every bit as uneasy as Tuckel felt. He was about to speak when several men stopped on the hotel porch and one came on through to the otherwise unoccupied dining-room. Sheriff McGee did not appear pleased to see Murch Chisum back in his town again, and that was exactly how he sounded as he spoke.

'I thought we'd seen the last of you, Mr Chisum.' He glanced suspiciously at the Treasury agent then back to the big man. 'Just what are you doing back here, investigator?'

'It's real good to see you again too, Sheriff,' Chisum said sarcastically. 'Mr Tuckel's pleased to see you too.'

McGee gave Tuckel a grudging nod.

'Has your return anything to do with last night's events, Mr Chisum?'

His manner was curt. Chisum the investigator had been involved in a shooting-scrape during his earlier visit, and that was enough to put him at odds with the sheriff. But there was a personal side also. Chloe Templeton and Chisum had been 'friends' during his visit. McGee disliked all the singer's male friends, especially rich ones like the undertaker or powerful ones like Chisum.

'Business, McGee,' Chisum replied, poker-faced. 'Strictly business. Sorry you're having all this trouble. Anything I can do to help?'

'Yes,' McGee snapped, turning on his heel. 'Stay right out of it.'

Chisum just shrugged as the peace officer strode from the room. He'd always been a high-stake player and didn't regard Chloe's tinstar admirer as someone of any real consequence. His focus had already returned to Brodie and the situation he'd created. It was simply not in Dodge City's top private investigator to stand by and watch opportunities slip away and not try and retrieve a given situation.

For the reality of this situation was that the true criminal here, as well as one of the least suspected, was Chisum himself.

From the moment he'd picked up the

scent of Hackman's brilliant plates, Murch Chisum had planned first to recover, then eventually utilize them. He had an overall plan to saturate the entire country with bogus banknotes and convert himself into a multi-millionaire overnight before Treasury or anyone else had the time or the acuity to realize what was happening.

The big man had been climbing all his life but that was his personal Everest. Chisum already knew where his thinking was leading him, but it still came as a shock to his companion when he said:

'I very much fear I'm going to have to disappoint Sheriff McGee. I can't stay out of the manhunt, Tuckel. Matter of fact I reckon I'm about to take it over.'

'What? What on earth are you talking about, man?'

Chisum met his eyes and held them with a look the other would not quickly forget.

'I think we are both aware of what should be done regarding Brodie, mister. There's no way out for him, guilty or innocent. If you and I are going to survive this mess, then get on with the business of running our counterfeiters to earth, then Brodie must simply be removed from the equation.'

Tuckel gasped.

'You're ... you're talking of eliminating the fellow?'

'Quick and neat,' responded Murchell Chisum, aware now that personal matters as well as professional were dominating his thinking. 'Don't look so shocked. I'm sure that is how Treasury likes you to handle untidy situations, Agent Tuckel?'

Tuckel just sat with his palms pressed flat against the table top, shocked but no longer protesting. For expedience was indeed a canon he was forced to live by, and the governmental mandarins high above him at least covertly subscribed to the theory that the ends justified the means anytime Uncle Sam's sacred monetary systems were considered at risk. In short, if it came to a choice between money and morality, money almost always won out.

'B-but, how will you find him if all those people have been unable to?' he asked, hating his weakness.

'Well, not by rifling chicken coops looking for footprints, let me assure you.' Chisum was rising and drawing on his gloves. 'You hired me as an investigator, remember? And that is what I do best of all. Investigate.'

Chloe wasn't concerned about his feet any

longer. For that matter, neither was Brodie himself now. He knew they would carry him wherever he wanted to go, now they were snug inside the pair of worn swamper's boots Chloe had lifted from Taggart's for him.

Footwear was uncomplicated. But how complicated was Chloe Templeton? He was pondering this as he rolled a Durham and studied her with a mixture of tenderness and puzzlement.

He'd known he was taking a long shot when he'd taken the huge risk of visiting the girl at her hotel via the outdoor stairs earlier, with half Morro out there sniffing after his scent and baying for his blood.

It was a huge gamble. Yet right from the outset, from the first moment he'd seen her singing and holding the saloon in thrall, he'd reacted to her on several different levels. Chloe Templeton was a heartbreaker and likely half the male population was crazy about her. She was also ambitious and had no compunction in attracting men and making sure they paid for the privilege.

But it was her third characteristic that drew him to take the risk of going to her, and it was significant. And that was her integrity. She might be showy, fickle and mercenary, yet he'd sensed in her a person to be trusted; that she possessed some world-weary yet warmhearted quality that told him she could prove a good friend – if you didn't try and treat her the way most men treated their women in rugged Morro – which he had not done.

So he'd gambled. And when he came looking for help she'd responded brilliantly. She'd actually acted more excited than endangered by his request for help, then had come up immediately with what was proving to be a superb and safe hideaway.

Although she had high opinions of herself and occasionally slipped information obtained from her 'friends' to others in order to help them or keep them from harm, down-to-earth Chloe had never seen herself as any kind of angel. She sang songs, dated different men, dreamed of bigger and better things and made compromises between her dreams and harsh reality.

But the notion of actually helping a fugitive on the run with a whole town howling for his blood was something totally new and had fired her imagination. And surely only a Chloe could or would dare have come up with the idea of seeking shelter in the sheriff's own storm cellar. It was secret, she had a key, and she insisted there was no risk of Cord McGee seeking the luxury of his refuge while 'killer' Brodie was still at large.

Brodie naturally felt immense gratitude towards someone who almost certainly had saved his life – or at least prolonged it.

But both soon realized she would eventually have to leave. If they noticed her missing, someone might just link them together – no telling where that could lead.

Brodie understood and accepted this, and made up his mind they should remain here together no longer than darkdown, then go their separate ways.

He had his own plans for the night, still some two hours away.

They spent the time talking like old friends, the investigator and the saloon girl, snug and secure beneath the sheriff's jailhouse. And after a couple of glasses of the lawman's wine, Chloe, finding something exhilarating in his quiet strength in his uniquely dangerous situation, began to talk as though they were old friends.

He learned she had started out with ambitions to become a singing star in Dodge City, Wichita, then right across the exploding West. Until experience taught her she was good, but not great. So she settled for a place like Taggart's in a town like Morro, and if men wanted to pursue her and shower her with gifts and money, why not? One day, maybe even soon, she would have enough put by to kick the dust of Morro off her heels and go north to make a real assault on the big time.

Or maybe Brodie thought all that sounded fanciful?

His reply was a chuckle.

For she had just outlined the life, times and frustrated ambitions of range detective Chad Brodie.

Now he understood why they'd seemed to be drawn to one another almost on sight. They were the same.

He told her so, and they were laughing and chatting like old friends before she eventually decided she must really go home to ready herself for the night's show at the hotel, a half-hour after the sun had set and darkness covered Morro County like a shroud.

He kissed her at the steps with genuine tenderness. Flighty, fickle, lovely Chloe had found him shelter from the storm. He hoped they both would still be alive come morning to celebrate that.

'You're a sweet, sweet man, Chad Brodie, and I know you wouldn't kill anyone who wasn't out to kill you.'

'Keep away from bad company, Chloe.' It was as though he were now saying goodbye for ever. Perhaps he was. For he intended quitting Morro but not the assignment. He never left a job unfinished. At last he'd figured out exactly the kind of place where a rancher and an undertaker might in safety print up bogus ten-dollar bills with beautiful plates 'donated' by a dead man. The conclusion he had drawn was the one he would follow up, even if Diamondback Ranch shaped up as about the unsafest place in Morro County for him at the moment.

Unless, of course, Jorge Achilles and his hardcase crew were all still here, away from base, searching for him.

The nickel had suddenly dropped on his flight back to Morro. Nobody but nobody was allowed onto Diamondback ranch. When you added that mystery to the fact that virtually all Achilles' crew was composed of hardcases and gunslingers rather than cowboys. Why hadn't he figured that one before?

His thoughts jolted back to the girl.

Moments before Chloe left he'd the impression there was something urgent she wanted to tell him, yet she'd left without a word and was quickly gone.

He rolled and lighted another cigarette before hauling on his swamper's boots. He grimaced with pain but reminded himself that sore feet were a joke compared to what might have befallen him that day.

He checked out his guns before turning out the light in the sheriff's hideaway.

Lauren Chisum could take care of herself. Her femininity was unchallengeable and she was strong and independent by nature. Her husband might have added she was also stubborn, temperamental, too fond of rye whiskey and possibly even sour on life itself, none of which criticisms were all that far from the truth. But, strengths and shortcomings notwithstanding, Chisum's lady was intelligent and perceptive and was driven by a strange old-fashioned morality. When Lauren chose Chisum as her husband and rejected his then junior apprentice, Chad Brodie, she was unashamedly motivated by ambition. Chisum was already a mover and shaker at that time, Brodie an ambitious nobody. She'd had her regrets since, but then most women do. She could live with that. But the demons that drove her today, as Morro relentlessly hunted Chad Brodie, had little to do with whom she loved or did not but rather stemmed from her perceptions along with her ever widening understanding of the man she was married to.

For deep down where her instincts lived, Lauren feared that when Chisum found time fully to assess the current Brodie situation here, he could and quite probably would decide his one-time protégé was a luxury he could no longer afford. She'd seen him make such brutal decisions before. This total ruthlessness was a prime part of the reason why Murchell Chisum had flourished while other investigators just received dunning letters from their landlords.

She hated it but had been able to live with it until someone she cared for was involved. Or should that be – more than just simply cared for, perhaps? She shook her head. She was far too old for Chad Brodie while in all likelihood he would always be too poor and unlucky for her.

So goes the world.

She was weary when she entered Taggart's saloon that night but certainly didn't look it. Indeed, she looked so good to the rangy cowpuncher who'd quit hunting fugitives for the night and had rolled up here with many like him to relax and hear Chloe sing and make them all feel better about their failure to bag Brodie, that he felt he just had to let his romantic side roam free.

'Hiya, honey!' he greeted boisterously, and grabbed her by the arm, detaining her. 'Whatever you're looking for, you've just found me.'

She simply stood motionless staring down at his hand on her arm. The cowboy began to redden and then his buddies started to snigger. She was so cool and superior that there was no way out for this rangeland Romeo but sheepishly to drop his arm and allow her to pass.

'Nice try,' she consoled him, then made her way through to the bar where drinkers made space for her.

The talk at Taggart's was all of the manhunt and by this time with tempers cooling and added information filtering through, it was now beginning to be suspected in many quarters that maybe Diamondback, not Brodie, had been responsible for the timberman's death. There were rumors that Achilles had set up an ambush for Brodie which had been aborted when their man came in from the west instead of down the ranch trail; that Brodie had been sighted on the stage trail; had floated downriver on a raft; that he was wounded and mostly likely had died. And – the wildest rumor of all – that Diamondback had caught him and strung him up and now would not admit it.

Small wonder Lauren craved a drink. Yet she didn't take one. Not today. Just coffee, thick and strong enough for the spoon to stand in it unsupported. She was always ready to drink to sandpaper her troubles away, but not this time. Not until she knew where Chad Brodie was, that he was all right.

In turn she chatted with cowboys and clerks, railroad personnel and storekeepers, those who believed Brodie was guilty and those who did not. On occasions during her restless search for a lead on the investigator's whereabouts – which in truth she never really expected to uncover – she had glimpsed her husband in full cry, covering Morro like a blanket, all high energy, intensity and laying on the charm or the authority, whichever he felt was required to get the lead he was seeking.

Usually so sure of herself, Chisum's world-weary wife was tonight confused, about her husband, Brodie and about herself. Why was she so desperate to find Chad before Chisum did? Did she really believe Chisum might feel he had to kill him? She had every right to be afraid, having come to know the man she was married to so well. But even if her fears for Brodie were justified, why didn't she do what she usually did at such times of tension and uncertainty in her life, namely sit back and take a drink or two?

She was still puzzling over this when she encountered the pretty blonde woman waiting for her cue to sing for the boys.

'Hello, I'm Chloe.' The woman introduced herself with a curious little smile dimpling her cheeks. 'You're Murch's wife, I hear tell. Funny thing, he didn't tell me he was married.'

CHAPTER 9

THE MONEY TRAIL

Priest closed the door on the room where two rapidly stiffening corpses lay on benches beneath tarpaulin covers. Business was booming but the undertaker was a man with far bigger concerns on his mind as his stare focused on Jorge Achilles' bulky shape leaning on his reception desk with a fuming cigar clenched between thick teeth.

'Anything fresh?' Priest's voice was roughened by fatigue and tension.

The cattleman glanced towards the front where the outlines of figures were dimly visible through frosted-glass doors.

'The boys are beat, so I brought them here with me to rest up some.'

'That the only reason?' Priest asked testily, making for the cabinet containing the smelling-salts and liquor set aside for grief-stricken clients. It wasn't the smelling-salts he was interested in.

'Meaning?' Achilles' manner was edgy. The counterfeiters were not weathering the ongoing manhunt for one fast-gun gravedigger well. Both had thrown all resources into the day-long manhunt for Brodie without success, and the coming of night found them weary and increasingly anxious. Maybe Brodie had gotten away? Maybe right now he was someplace spilling his guts to some lawman on what really happened on the Diamondback?

It had occurred to both men that if Brodie was able to make contact with Deacon's head man, Jackson, already deeply suspicious of Diamondback's account of Joe's death – they could expect big trouble from the clannish timbermen. Now, to compound matters further, Murch Chisum was back in town, involving himself in matters that did not concern him.

'Maybe you thought you might have wanted your hardcases on hand close by in case something went awry,' Priest replied, splashing brandy into two glasses.

'Such as?' Achilles was belligerent. He always was when under pressure. Yet real pressure for these two partners in crime had been rare until now. They'd enjoyed a dream run with their secret money-manufacturing enterprise right up to the day Chad Brodie showed up at the parlor looking for work. Now they drank brandy straight and started at every loud noise from the street.

'Such as having them close to hand in case we need them,' Priest said grimly. Big globules of sweat trickled down Achilles' beefy face. He drained his glass and held it out for a refill. Neither man spoke for a long time.

It had all begun on a night much like this with two long-time pards having a quiet after-hours drink in the gloomy hush of Priest's somber place of business. Priest had been in a strange kind of mood that night, watchful, tense and radiating a kind of suppressed excitement. This puzzled the rancher. They went a long way back, and if there was one thing Priest never displayed, it had to be excitement. Everyone said he was born with formaldehyde in his veins and his big smooth face seemed set permanently into sympathetic lines.

By contrast, Achilles was loud and aggressive and in his usual booming, half-belligerent mood as he swallowed down his first glass and crossed to the bottle shelf to pour another.

That was when he saw the intricately etched metallic plates just lying there uncovered upon the shelf directly beneath the light, where he couldn't help but see them.

He swung to stare at a no-longer solemn undertaker, who straightaway challenged the big man to remind him of what both had been thinking, dreaming and planning of every single day since Priest had gone to a humpy in the back hills to collect Hackman's effects – and discovered a ticket to millions hidden away in a rough canvas sack.

The plates were dynamite, they knew.

Counterfeiting had broken out in the county south of Dodge the previous year; then suddenly ceased. Only the Diamondhead boss and his undertaker friend knew both the who and the why of that incident. Hackman had been the brilliant counterfeiter, and the rash of forged notes dried up when he passed on.

And that was the night when Priest made a huge decision; when, after weeks of the two of them doing nothing and saying not much more to one another about the plates, Wilson Priest set up the stage with the plates on display as a prelude to his proposal.

Namely, did Achilles dare make the leap from hard times, poor cattle prices and freezing his ass off every Plains winter in that ramshackle Diamondback ranch house – and take Dame Fortune's hand; say goodbye for ever to hard times and empty pockets and give a welcome to riches?

That was how the pedantic Priest phrased his proposal. What the man meant, of course, was that should they quit griping about hard times and set about making themselves rich, courtesy of the late and, in one way at least, great Tanner Hackman.

Even now, Achilles felt warmed and strengthened by memories of that night which had led to them setting up their secret printery, mastering the rogue's art in double quick time and ultimately going on to spread the counterfeit Achilles-Priest product far and wide.

Achilles now brought himself back to the reality of the here and now. Their first whiff of a threat had been a month earlier when the renowned Dodge City investigator, Murch Chisum had shown up with a hard-faced young assistant looking for the source of a flow of counterfeit ten-dollar bills.

Chisum had scared the hell out of them. Then he got into that shooting scrape at Frog Hollow, was creased and soon after disappeared.

The partners halted production for two weeks, then quietly went back to printing money. They'd grown accustomed to their big houses, fine wines and pretty women and were totally committed to surviving, to secrecy, to dealing if necessary with anyone they perceived as threatening their oper-ation in any way.

Their set-up was carefully planned and rigidly overseen, and in time the impact of the Chisum scare began to fade. Recently both seemed to sense some undercurrent of threat with odd things happening that they couldn't quite explain. They put it down to nerves, reinforcing one another's commitment. There could be no turning back, no regrets, just iron determination to see this period through and come out on top, like always. Rich winners.

So they talked and drank until eventually the cattleman, always concerned for security at headquarters, made the fateful decision to spend what was left of the night hunting Brodie rather than return with his men to Diamondback to guard their glittering assets.

He wanted to leave a note of thanks but could not take the risk in case McGee might find it before she did. He didn't even know if Chloe would return to the cellar room, but even if she did, he would be long gone.

He was quitting his unlikely sanctuary and heading back to Diamondback.

He was definite about that now as he shrugged into his jacket, the reflection of his features in the bookcase's glass doors showing a grim-faced man with tight white lines cutting the corners of his mouth.

Small wonder he looked that way, he reflected.

Outside he would be risking a town crawling with people hunting for him. He must steal a horse and get away unseen, then make his way out to the spread which, he was hoping, he would find undermanned and vulnerable tonight.

Now he grinned stiffly at his reflection. He could not be sure if he was doing some excellent deductive work here, or was just grabbing at straws. He only knew it was time to find out, one way or another.

For the longer he thought of the kind of space, equipment and security a professional counterfeit gang would require to maintain both production and safety, coupled with his bloody brushes with Achilles' gunmen – not cowhands – the more convinced he became that it had to be up there on the plateau, someplace out of sight and under guard with Jorge Achilles in command.

He was ultra cautious in easing up the cellar stairs, locking the storm cellar doors and secreting the key where Chloe had shown him. She had insisted that the sheriff would be far too busy for his books and solitude during the hunt, and that was how it had panned out.

If he ever got to relate the story of how he had hidden under the lock-up itself in a town baying for his blood, he would try and make it a good one.

Nobody expected fugitive Chad Brodie to be seen tramping boldly down the middle of the main street shrouded beneath a tugged-down hat and greatcoat, which was the very reason he was able to get away with it. Quietly and expertly stealing a horse on a street lined with crowded hitch racks proved similarly uneventful. There was one bad moment when a drunk with a rifle challenged him as he rode across the railroad tracks, but he called back:

'Sorry, can't stop. Running an errand for the sheriff!' And the man with the gun waved him on his way.

By the time he had covered Blackwood Street and two of the three main saloons, Chisum felt he knew one hell of a lot more about his quarry than he had on starting out. Such as what Brodie had done during his stretch here, whom he'd shared time with, what the man in the street really thought about him.

He knew, for instance, that Brodie had made a big impression up at Deacon, yet privately rejected the Diamondback version of their clashes with his man. He was also aware that both Wilson Priest and even the sheriff had thought highly of Brodie right until the shoot-out up on Diamondback.

He also knew now that Brodie had not spent all his nights here alone, propping up a bar stool.

Chisum halted directly across the street from Taggart's saloon. Somehow he was not surprised to learn that Chloe had befriended Brodie. She was the type who loved the new and the different, as he'd discovered during their brief friendship on his original visit. She was a knockout and they'd had a few good times together. Yet his interest in her had mainly been as a source of information about Morro and its citizens as he'd searched for his counterfeiters. It was due to her friendship with Priest, her 'sugar-daddy' as she called him, that she had let slip to Chisum about 'something strange' going on at Frog Hollow. In turn this had led to his riding out there with two juniors as part of his investigation. This had erupted into a shoot-out with employees eventually identified as hands of both Priest and Achilles, who ever since had been the investigator's number one suspects.

A sudden thought: maybe Chloe knew something about Brodie's whereabouts? He'd uncovered the fact that they were 'close', whatever the hell that might mean.

He supposed Brodie was her type – young, handsome and a loser. Chloe had let Murch Chisum spend money on her, and she had something ongoing with old moneybags Priest. But underneath he suspected she favored those more of her own class.

He strode across the street and shouldered his way inside, only to he halted almost immediately by the law.

'Just a minute, Chisum,' Cord McGee said, his voice hoarse with weariness. 'I think it's about time you explained what your stake in this whole affair might be, don't you? I've seen you running yourself ragged all afternoon stirring up people all over about Brodie and I want to know why.'

Chisuin was not listening. He was staring off in back where the two prettiest women in Morro were seated at a table over coffee, deep in animated conversation.

'Shit!' he said and strode off leaving the peeved lawman staring after him.

Chloe and Lauren glanced up as he reached their table, the former cheerful as always but his wife had an odd look in her eye.

'Whatever she's told you, forget it,' he snapped at the singer.

'It's all right, darling,' Lauren said

smoothly, and he was surprised to find her sober at nine o'clock at night. 'You don't have to play the big bold investigator with little old us.' She smiled up at him brilliantly. 'Chloe and I were just discussing Chad, our mutual friend.'

The man paled. His wife always had the ability to throw him off balance. Sometimes she was too much for him. He would never admit it to a living soul, but it was the truth.

But Chloe Templeton was something entirely different. He knew the singer and understood her bright, fickle temperament. She used men, not the other way round. He already knew she'd become tight with Brodie, and again he was reminded that his man would be exactly the kind of fellow who would genuinely attract her, as distinct from her Daddy Big Bucks admirers. Including himself. Suddenly his mind was racing, with his instincts kicking in when he started figuring just who a man of Brodie's caliber might be tempted to turn to in a place where he'd scarcely had time enough to make more than two or three friends.

He excelled at this sort of deduction. He had, after all, climbed to the peak of the sleuthing profession, before turning his ambitions to higher and more dangerous things.

When Chloe eventually quit Taggart's that night to make her way along Blackwood where foot-weary men were still going through the motions of hunting for Brodie, he knew exactly where she was heading when she turned into Oak Street. He'd walked her to her hotel several times. When she vanished inside he found himself a comfortable spot out of the cold and smoked a cigar, tapping one foot on the plankwalk boards.

It was a half-hour later when a slim, shrouded figure emerged and hurried west. He flipped his cigar butt into the street and followed.

Achilles territory.

As far as a man could see and every bit as dark and menacing as a man with imagination could make at a moment that simply breathed danger, Diamondback's gloomy acres surrounded him in the big night.

A dim pacing figure rose up out of the gullywash south of the homestead where the lights were dim and the silhouette of a slow-moving sentry moved past a window.

Brodie breathed shallowly, snuffing the air like a hunting animal as he stood motionless with boots planted on Diamondback dirt beneath a whispering old cedar, soaked up by the night.

His gun was in his hand and his horse was a mile away beyond the boundary fence. Almost everything he saw and heard reassured him that the spread was every bit as normal, quiet and peaceful as any cattle outfit should be this time of night.

But he was betting big that he would find the Diamondback was anything but regular. He might even be betting his life on finding out.

He shook his head and prepared to wait some more. He wasn't about to take any reckless chances, wouldn't move until he'd gotten the feel of enemy country. He was certain it had to be that. Even if Achilles wasn't the counterfeiter he certainly was the enemy. The rancher had shown his bloody hand before, and Brodie knew that if they should come face to face here on the big man's grass it could prove ugly. Calmly, coldly, he knew if it came to a showdown he would take Achilles down the way that fat bastard had done Deacon Joe. He hoped it mightn't come to that. On the ride out he was convinced he'd identified the forgers and wanted both alive to spill everything, to help him cross the Ts and dot the Is before a judge and jury.

As his eyes became accustomed to the darkness he was able to pick out the shapes and positions of barns, corrals, meathouse and tackrooms, all shrouded and silent.

Eventually he glimpsed another dim light. He frowned and took a dozen paces forward to look again. From that point he could make out the silhouetted outline of another high-shouldered barn some distance south of the house, and it was from there that the muted light was showing.

His pulse picked up a beat.

If the counterfeiters were set up here, as he figured, then they would need someplace sizable and solid to work. A big old ranch barn would be ideal. Taking a fresh grip on his sixshooter he began skirting the other buildings and making his silent way south. The sentry was where he'd expected to find him. But who but a greenhorn would stand on a high pommel of land where he was outlined against the sky?

The dark figure paced towards him.

Brodie clawed a pebble from the ground. He flipped it in a low arc. It landed behind the pacing man. He turned sharply, started in the direction of the sound, and the shadow was closing in.

One blow of the barrel was all it took. The waddy grunted and Brodie lowered him silently to the buffalo grass, then went streaking for the barn.

A knot-hole in a side wall revealed the lights, the long table littered with piles of paper and bank-notes, the printing equipment. He was staring one-eyed at what was plainly a fully equipped and working counterfeit operation!

There was no time for jubilation. Four men were visible, two in inkstained coveralls, obviously the printers, and another two of the Diamondback's hardcases he'd seen in Morro and during the ambuscade.

His stare focused on the gleaming plates in the old-fashioned printing-machine under a hanging light, and he took a long swallow.

Solid odds.

But what had he expected?

It didn't take long to find the door.

The counterfeiters had the numbers but the silent intruder had the edge. It was late, the men didn't want to be working while the rest of the crew was in Morro looking to blow that bastard Brodie out of his boots. The first sentry was actually yawning and massaging watery eyes when a gunbutt came down on him and sent him spinning into blackness.

As sleek and purposeful as a hunting cat, a low-crouching Brodie sprang forward as the second gunman heard something and whirled. The man's eyes popped wide and he was jerking up a Big Fifty rifle real fast as the gap between them closed. The sixgun barrel was quicker and man and rifle hit the board floor.

The bone-weary printers blinked as though he was some kind of apparition as he came forward. They were small-time crooks with certain skills, imported by Achilles and the undertaker, not to beef up security but specifically to operate the presses.

They were accustomed to working around dangerous men, but this stranger with the cocked Colt in his fist, travel-stained, cold-eyed and wolflike in the yellow light had them shaking and, without even being ordered, they slowly raised their hands.

'Talk!' Chad hissed. 'I don't have much time.'

The smaller of the two men was too scared to talk. He'd been virtually hijacked into this operation by his redheaded partner, and even though a lifetime crook and counterfeiter with prison time behind him, he'd found Diamondback and almost everybody on it from Achilles down scary and intimidating. The sudden appearance of this cold-eyed man with the sixshooter scared him most of all, and he looked appealingly to his partner for help.

The redhead fancied himself as a tough guy. Glaring defiantly, he clamped his lips tight, folded his arms – then next moment hit the floor.

Brodie had struck so fast he hadn't even seen it coming. Reefed to his feet and slapped hard, he started talking like he didn't know how to stop.

The story that unfolded fitted in pretty well within the ambit of how Brodie'd figured it had to be; Hackman died, the undertaker came by his plates, two long-time pards decided to make a grab for the good life, and had plainly been doing just fine, or at least right up to this eye-locked moment.

Brodie grunted in satisfaction.

He wanted to hear more but every additional minute he spent here added to his risk. Likely by this Achilles could have figured he wasn't going to find their quarry in town tonight, and might well be heading for the home acres.

He barked orders and the pair filled a gunny sack with a huge bundle of ten-dollar bills and the plates. The frightened little man passed him the sack and Brodie rewarded him with a short hard thump on the head that dropped him cold.

'He's the lucky one,' he warned the redhead. 'You're coming with me to repeat to the law just what you told me or you're a dead man. *Sabe?*'

He clicked the gun hammer and the man went white. Brodie was laying it on with a trowel. He had to. He was far from out of the woods yet and he wanted the printer so scared he wouldn't be game to look sideways.

All was still quiet as he prodded his catch through the side door with his gunbarrel, cache slung over one shoulder, already calculating how long it would take his double-laden horse to get them down to Morro. And then, how he might get to reach the sheriff with his hostage, with his proof, his prisoner and himself all still in one piece in that angry town.

He calculated he'd taken no more than three steps when he realized that the old barn's thick walls had been muffling the sound of approaching horses. Disbelieving, he propped to see dark riders flooding in off the main trail, faint starlight glinting off metal trim, spurs and guns.

'That's him! There he is!'

The shout was drowned out by the crash of the first shot, but not before he'd recognized the triumphant roar of the big man leading them in.

He was stunned.

It wasn't Achilles or even Wilson Priest, but Chisum!

He barely made it back inside before the bullets began raining down like hail.

CHAPTER 10

SHADE OF ODDS

The redhead was ashen with terror as a howling slug found its way through a chink higher up and ricocheted around the barn like a demented hard-shelled insect before dropping smoking onto the work bench.

'They're gonna kill all of us!' he bleated. 'Why us? Are you gonna just let 'em murder us, Brodie? We ain't done nothin'.'

'Shut up and keep low!'

Brodie's bark was flat and harsh as he

clambered up steps leading to the hayloft where a window was out. He held his reloaded Colt in one hand and the sentry's Big Fifty in the other.

The shouting outside could barely be heard above the snarling volleys but the voices were excited, almost hysterical. He'd seen enough to realize Chisum had shown up with some six or seven towners who looked like they'd been recruited from the back-street bars, then supplied with horses, weapons and maybe even booze for courage.

Bums. But any bum with a gun was dangerous. But how in the hell had Chisum known he'd find him here? It seemed next door to impossible that the man could have done it.

He shook his head and concentrated. Time for questions later, if there was a later. The way those shadowy riders were hooting and hollering, Chisum must have primed them on plenty of liquor and big talk on the trail out. Right at that moment his long dedication to the range detective's life was looking a little shaky. Right now, he could be working safe and happy at the poker-tables in Warrior Creek.

'Here they come!' screeched the little forger, brought round by all the commotion, his bulging eyes to a chink. 'Glory, don't them boys know we're in here, Red?'

The redhead's response was lost in the bellow of a big gun. Lead ploughed into plank walls, bored its way through, crashed through bottles, pans and printing machinery.

Brodie cursed as he took aim. He'd hoped the walls would prove stronger. But hope wouldn't boil beans. He lined up a racing figure with his sixgun and gently squeezed trigger. Nothing fancy here. A sound, workmanlike job of killing was all that stood between him and total disaster right now.

The rider took his bullet in the gut and spilled from the saddle, bouncing beneath the hoofs of a cowboy's cayuse, then rolling away, his agonized screeching working on nerves like the rasp of a bone-saw.

Resting his gun on the sill, Brodie calmly triggered again and shot another man out of his saddle. Yet still they came, screaming and shooting like Quahadi Comanches, and suddenly a slug snoring by his ear warned that they'd spotted his position.

He instantly dropped low and darted to an aperture behind the rear door. No time to figure out how or why Chisum got to be leading this bunch, or why the bastard seemed so dead-set on murdering him now. Time only to fight. He was cool, knew he was shooting better than he'd ever done in his life. Yet they still had the numbers, and now invisible hands were employing something heavy and solid to batter at the double doors at the building's far end.

Was this, after all, about to prove to be both his biggest job and his last? His jaws set tight as a beaver-trap and slitted eyes blazed anger and something more. Outrage. Chisum had set him up; Chisum was the criminal here – no other explanation was possible.

Cocking the big gun he stared out at a nightmare scene where the icy dark was held at bay by blazing brands and flaring guns, the gunsmoke hanging like hoar-frost on buildings, barns and huge and solemn trees.

The world he might be leaving.

Might.

Win or lose, he would make it cost them. Maybe he'd even go under without too much griping if he could first hammer a .50 .50 slug from the big rifle through Chisum's rotten heart.

A scream distracted him as he hefted the big weapon. The redhead had ripped open a side door and was immediately struck. The man tottered backwards with tight little steps, trying to hold his insides in. As he tumbled sideways to his death, the voice of Chisum rose above the tumult.

'In you go now, boys! Earn your money while I cover you. We'll all cover you. And remember, a thousand dollars to the man who nails the gravedigger!'

Moments later the doors at the far end caved in under the battery of a heavy post and and two lean gunmen came lurching into the light with sixshooters blazing.

He fired the Big Fifty from waist-level. A man threw up his arms and fell backwards with a hoarse cry to disappear through the doorway. The second was a mean-looking heller who got a shot away that was so wild Brodie didn't even have to duck. The rifle belched smoke and death again and the backstreet hardcase collapsed to the floor in the foetal position, clutching his belly and screaming like a woman.

Yet still they came, and a ducking and shooting Brodie was counting his life in mere moments now that the defences had been completely breached. He thought briefly of Chloe and Lauren, even had a passing warm thought for Warrior Creek and his shabby little up-a-flight office. Funny, but he'd always expected to make it big before the end. Showed you how wrong you could be.

Then he heard it. Despite gunfire, wild shouting and the screams of the desperately wounded, his battle-deafened ears were still able to identify the underlay of drumming sounds that caused him to listen hard and feel the sudden improbable kick of hope.

Hoofbeats!

But even before he could identify the sounds beyond all doubt, the pessimism hit. Sure, horsemen. But what reason did he have to expect they'd be his? Who in hell would know he was out here with armed madmen howling for his blood? And if anyone did know, why would they care?

His heart felt stopped by dust.

Yet even as he prepared for the end his subconscious was sending him urgent signals. He could still hear the surge of hoofs and the grunting of hard-ridden horses, yet not one rider had as yet shown himself.

His head cocked sharply, eyes widening. What was happening out there? Who attacked a building on horseback when a smashed-in door was an open invitation just to walk in shooting?

Crouched behind two grease-drums, he

focused fiercely on the double doorway, but still nobody appeared, mounted or otherwise. The uproar outside had swelled to an avalanche of warlike sounds, gunfire, screaming, and still the surge of horses.

Then the voice that cut through it all:

'Throw down your weapons or you're all done for, scum!' followed by the hard spang of a Spencer rifle.

He couldn't stay put any longer.

He rushed to the doorway in a crouch and stared out into the smoky night in time to see a horse go scorching by dragging a screaming man by the stirrup – a Diamondback man.

He grunted in astonishment. The ranch yard was filled with horsemen and by the moonlight he realized now they were Deacon men, long, rangy riders on pintos blasting away with old-fashioned weapons that filled the night with smoke and death.

Relief flooded over him as he sagged against the jamb. He couldn't even begin to figure what had brought the timbermen in, didn't need to know. All that signified was that Jackson and his boys had arrived just in time. It should have been over quickly but someone was urging the Morro men to fight back, someone with a booming voice he recognized. He'd find out if he was right or wrong later – if there was a later for him.

Then: 'Brodie! Watch your back, man!'

That voice was familiar. He jerked his head round to make out the familiar lean figure of Sheriff Cord McGee, star glinting on his chest, riding stirrup to stirrup with clan leader Jackson as they emerged from the mêlée some thirty feet distant. Both were pointing at something in back of him.

He instantly spun on his heels to see danger bursting clear of wild-eyed horses and raging men to come galloping towards him, a big man whose pale face was set in a demonic mask of total rage and whose hand held a bucking sixshooter. Shooting at him.

Chisum.

In that instant Brodie the detective was Brodie the fighter again. As his Colt whipped up and a bullet fanned white-hot past his cheek, he was a tougher, angrier Brodie than he'd ever been, outraged by treachery and intent on survival.

He triggered and kept shooting until the big body buckled and was belted backwards over the saddle to strike earth with a brutal thud. It rolled through dirty snow almost to the stoop, the riderless horse, mad with fear, missing Brodie's smoke-shrouded figure by inches.

The attack collapsed in that moment. For it was Chisum and his money that had brought the Morro trash into this fight. He hadn't let them quit when the Deacon men attacked, but now he couldn't stop them. Judging by the way Chisum had struck ground he would be a lucky man ever to get to stop or start anything again.

Slowly the shooting faded and fearful towners and triumphant timbermen were calming their horses and turning their full attention to the tableau by the barn wall, where Brodie had moved slowly to stand now above the face that flared up at him from the slush: bloodless, ashy-gray and full of hate.

'Why?'

It was a simple question. Why had Chisum come to kill him? Why attack the ranch? Why?

'It was going to be all mine, loser!' Chisum's voice was powerful no longer, just one rub above a whisper. An irregular thunder beat in his ears and a whitish lightning hurt his eyes. 'You were going to find the plates to make me rich, then as soon as you did you were always going to die because you would know too much.'

His face twisted as the full terrifying agony

gripped him and when he continued his voice was weaker. Now he was staring past Brodie as though seeing a vision.

'It was like a dream when I saw Hackman's first dodgy ten-dollar bill that day. Sure ... I'd gone to the top ... but was only part-way where I'd always wanted to be. Those big tycoons you saw come to Dodge to hire me ... they were truly rich and I hated their guts for it. But when I saw that note, a note only a Treasury expert could tell was crooked, I knew I would find those plates some day, print ten million dollars' worth and spread them all over the country before anyone knew what was going on and nobody would ever know...'

He broke off, coughing blood.

Brodie's face was stone.

'So you sent me in to find them for you. But then what? You'd knew I'd turn the plates over to Tuckel.'

'Sure you would, you sanctimonious bastard. Only you wouldn't have been around to do anything, would you?'

Brodie nodded understandingly.

'You'd have had me killed,' he said slowly. 'Just for a set of plates.'

Somehow Chisum struggled to raise himself on one elbow.

211

'Mainly for that, but not just for that. I hated your guts from the first, mister. You with your honest Injun ways and honesty and holier-than-thou bullshit. And, of course, my wife. She took one look at you and realized straight away you were the range dick she should've latched onto ... not big bad Chisum...'

'Lauren? What are you talking about? We're just friends.'

'Like you and Chloe are just friends?' Chisum shook violently and slumped back into the mud. Then a savage grin. 'I figured about you and her ... tonight. So I tracked her to your hidy-hole ... had to really get tough with her, make her 'fess up where you'd gone. No ... no trouble to round up a mob to go after the timberman's killer...'

His eyes widened. 'I could have had it all...' His voice broke off and his head rolled until only mere slits of his eyes showed through smoke-smudged lids, still flaring with hate and a hungry greed. Next moment he was gone and Brodie unknotted his bandanna and spread it over his face.

'Well,' declared the silver-haired county commissioner as the in-camera three-day preliminary hearing into the counterfeiting

212

ring drew towards a close, 'it would appear that about the only people to come through this whole grotesque and sorry affair would be two brave and praiseworthy ladies – and of course, our hero of the day, detective Chad Brodie.'

'Hmmph!' Brodie muttered to himself. He wasn't being disrespectful, for the commissioner had been meticulously thorough and proficient in uncovering all the facts and building a crystal-clear composite picture of all that had taken place since the Hackman plates had fallen into the hands of the undertaker, right up to the present, which saw Chisum in his dishonorable grave and Wilson Priest and Jorge Achilles locked in the sheriff's cells until their trial day came around the following week.

No, this investigator couldn't complain about anything here at the hearing which had also revealed the vital roles Chloe and Lauren had played in the final result. Today, Chloe still sported bandaged arms, testimony to the torture Chisum had inflicted upon her in the sheriff's hideaway, after cleverly and correctly figuring that the girl might be privy to Brodie's whereabouts. But she still looked glamorous, while Lauren Chisum wasn't even wearing widow's black.

If Chisum was missed it wasn't evident in this conference room at the courthouse.

The wife's testimony had been illuminating.

She drew a vivid word-picture of the changes that had overcome her husband from the very moment he caught the first whiff of Hackman and his plates. He'd nursed a lifelong determination to become genuinely rich and powerful and she realized, in the end, that he'd instantly visualized the counterfeit engravings as the key by which it could be achieved.

It was fitting that Cord McGee should draw his full share of official kudos for the manner in which he'd formed a posse and led it, and Brodie was even more grateful to the man who'd saved his life.

Towards the end of the hearing, Brodie felt himself getting just a little peeved, for a reason only he understood.

The reason had a name. Money.

Most of his troubles had always been with money. Everyone agreed he'd played the major role in busting up the counterfeit ring, even the county commissioner and his legal staff had stated so officially. In addition, he had also exposed Chisum's hitherto unsuspected secret plan to gain possession of the

Hackman plates and eventually flood America with vast amounts of fake money of such quality that it could have ruined the economy.

This was surely big-league territory and he'd been the star player.

He'd reckoned there would at least be a reward – but not a *centavo*. After listening to Treasury Agent Tuckel praise him to the skies at the hearing he'd figured he might count on a monetary governmental recognition of his work. But no dice. It appeared the gentlemen who daily dealt in millions for their country were more tight-fisted than Scrooge.

Newsmen interviewed him, women fawned over him; he was a hero up in Deacon. But did that translate into dollars and cents? No way.

But he'd managed to thrust such material thoughts aside by the time he sat down to a farewell supper at the Morro Hotel with two brave and beautiful women to whom he was deeply and happily in debt.

During the hearing it was revealed how, sensing justice could be closing in on the counterfeiters, and aware of the singer's friendship with Brodie, Chisum had tracked her to the sheriff's safe house, then used a knife to torture her into revealing that Brodie had hinted at his suspicion of Diamondback. Somehow the injured girl had made her way to the saloon where her new friend Lauren Chisum took care of her, then had the courage and presence of mind to go directly to the sheriff, who in turn had galloped post-haste to Deacon, knowing he'd have no trouble in rounding up a posse to accompany him to the hated Diamondback.

By this time Chisum had rounded up his own bunch of Poor Town hotheads and headed post-haste for the spread with the double intention of gaining possession of the plates and ridding himself of Brodie before he succeeded in uncovering his criminal plans.

Brodie totally supported the glowing remarks on the two women by the county commissioner, and secretly wished he might get to spend a lot more time with either or both. But that simply wasn't possible. Chad Brodie was certainly some kind of hero now, yet still broke and couldn't show anyone a good time. On the other hand, Lauren and Chloe were handsome courageous women, sure, but both loved the high life and already had big plans to go up to Dodge

216

together, pool their resources and go into the fashion business together.

They urged him to join them as business manager, protector and whatever else he might think of. It was a dizzyingly tempting offer, but a man had his pride. Besides, he was still what he'd always been, a range detective, and a range detective he would stay.

He still recalled that memorable day in Chisum's big office when silver-headed tycoons in railroads, beef, gold and silver kept upping the bids for his services. If that could happen to one investigator, surely it could happen to another.

In the meantime he would enjoy the reality of Chisum gone, Achilles and Priest being held for trial, the spectacle of life slowly but surely returning to normal in Morro County – and he was being treated to a bang-up supper by two of the loveliest ladies in all Kansas.

Surely life could be a lot tougher than that?

Surely life couldn't be tougher than this?

It was a grungy gray day with a thin rain trying hard not to fall as Warrior Peak's hero detective trudged up the rickety outside stairs to his office above the tailor's shop. He was surprised to find that his door still opened to his key, considering a spiteful letter he'd found in his letterbox from B.B.B. and Associates, threatening him with eviction.

Inside, he stood staring down at the letter that had been slipped underneath the door. Another one. They always used the same cheap envelopes. He sighed and thought wearily:

'Welcome home, Brodie. You clean up the Morro counterfeit ring almost single handedly, receive a hero's farewell over there and another here at the Creek. Yet at the end of it all you finish up even further behind the eight ball than ever.'

What a crock!

He was tempted to ignore the letter but in the end curiosity won out. He ripped it open to read;

We despise tardy tenants. But we are true Americans who honor our heroes.
All arrears hereby cancelled.

He almost grinned. Maybe things had changed? Experience warned him not to read the postscript. But what the heck?

Leaking roof your responsibility.
Attend forthwith or else.

Like they said. Everything changes, everything remains the same.

He poured himself a shot and carried it to the window. He supposed he was half-amused by it all, yet as he stood sipping and listening to the plumbing gurgling down below, he realized that maybe it was time to face up to reality.

He knew he'd done a quality job in Morro, which had reinforced his confidence in his abilities. But if a man couldn't get some kind of professional boost after hitting the front pages territory-wide as he'd done, when could he expect it? It grew quieter and quieter, colder and colder. He returned to the cabinet for another jolt, loosened his string tie, slumped in his sagging chair behind the battered desk and began thinking about sheriffing, security work, maybe acting as a bodyguard for some bloated bigwig who would treat him like a son and pay him ... peanuts, most likely.

He grimaced sourly and with the rain on the tin roof didn't hear the footsteps on the stairs. Didn't even notice at first when she walked in.

She was blonde and beautiful and her legs seemed to go on for ever. She wore a shimmering silk dress with a fox stole over one shoulder and walked across his mean little room like a queen on her way to her coronation, smiling back at him with lips like crushed cherries.

He stared at the drink in his hand. He had to be hallucinating.

Then: 'Mr Brodie? Mr Chad Brodie, the famous range detective, recently of Morro?'

This was no illusion. Why hadn't he bothered to put on a fresh shirt? And shaved?

'Ma'am?' he got out. 'Or, er, Miss? Yeah, I'm Brodie.'

He was never this awkward. He was just taken aback, was all.

She thrust out a kid-gloved hand.

'Angelina Salisbury of the Kansas and London Salisburys. A pleasure. Do meet Mummy, Daddy and my Uncle Bertie Thrushmore of the Boston Thrushmores. Darlings, this is the renowned Mr Brodie.'

'Damned proud to shake your hand, sir,' insisted the monocled uncle. Then he squeezed Brodie's shoulder and nodded approvingly to the enormous gentleman in the vast beaver coat and smiled hugely.

'Sound as the US dollar. Tell me, are your services available, sir?'

'Huh?' Brodie wondered if it was a gag. Maybe not.

'Er, yes,' he replied, catching some of his balance now. 'Available...'

He broke off as the mustachioed uncle slapped a wad of notes on the desk.

'Five hundred American dollars retainer.'

'We broke our eastward journey at Dodge City to take train down here after reading of your amazing exploits at Morro,' the elegant Angelina informed him, perching on the edge of his desk and swinging one long, lissom leg. 'You see, our wealthy aunt in Kansas City passed on during our absence in Nevada, in strange circumstances...'

'Murdered?' Brody asked, always the detective.

'We don't know,' her father said grimly, a big ruddy-faced man with a mane of silver hair. 'But circumstances were dubious. You see, we have a whole gaggle of sly and avaricious nieces and nephews who may or not have hastened her demise. These same relatives have powerful connections in Wichita and we're not at all sure about the law there. But when we read about your exploits, your cleverness, courage and devotion to duty, why we all agreed instantly and unanimously that we should come visit and ask you to assist us to unravel this regrettable matter. Er, do you wish to hear more, Mr Brodie?'

He couldn't reply, could only shake his head.

He was gaping and knew it. It was his wildest dream come true. A mystery and possible crime such as a man like himself only ever read about, rich and important clients, a beautiful young woman and, by the sound of it, the chance to put up his gun and buckle down to some genuine, high-grade detective work, away from these damned prairies for a change.

It only needed one thing to make it perfect, and, as though reading his mind, Uncle Bertie cleared his throat and said the magic words:

'Money no object, of course.'

He was their man!

THE END

The publishers hope that this book has given you enjoyable reading. Large Print Books are especially designed to be as easy to see and hold as possible. If you wish a complete list of our books please ask at your local library or write directly to:

Dales Large Print Books
Magna House, Long Preston,
Skipton, North Yorkshire.
BD23 4ND

This Large Print Book, for people
who cannot read normal print,
is published under the auspices of

THE ULVERSCROFT FOUNDATION